By Royal Appointment

You're invited to a royal wedding!

From turreted castles to picturesque palaces,
these kingdoms may be steeped in tradition,
but romance always rules!

So don't miss your VIP invite to the most
extravagant weddings of the year!

Your royal carriage awaits....

Look out for your next invitation to a royal wedding:

Princess Australia
by
Nicola Marsh
Harlequin Romance, coming in June

"What kind of a king are you?"

"Certainly not the one my father envisioned," Alex responded. "I plan to be your husband in every sense of the word. I want another child."

"What if I can't?" Darrell's voice squeaked.

"Have children, you mean?"

"No. I meant, what if I can't marry you?"

A remote expression crossed over his rugged features. "In that case I'll have to surrender the throne."

"You can't abdicate. This is your life. There are too many people depending on you. You can't do it. I won't let you do it."

"Good. Then we'll say our vows in the chapel, tonight."

REBECCA WINTERS

Matrimony with His Majesty

By Royal Appointment

HARLEQUIN®

TORONTO • NEW YORK • LONDON
AMSTERDAM • PARIS • SYDNEY • HAMBURG
STOCKHOLM • ATHENS • TOKYO • MILAN • MADRID
PRAGUE • WARSAW • BUDAPEST • AUCKLAND

If you purchased this book without a cover you should be aware that this book is stolen property. It was reported as "unsold and destroyed" to the publisher, and neither the author nor the publisher has received any payment for this "stripped book."

ISBN-13: 978-0-373-03944-9
ISBN-10:   0-373-03944-1

MATRIMONY WITH HIS MAJESTY

First North American Publication 2007.

Copyright © 2007 by Rebecca Winters.

All rights reserved. Except for use in any review, the reproduction or utilization of this work in whole or in part in any form by any electronic, mechanical or other means, now known or hereafter invented, including xerography, photocopying and recording, or in any information storage or retrieval system, is forbidden without the written permission of the publisher, Harlequin Enterprises Limited, 225 Duncan Mill Road, Don Mills, Ontario, Canada M3B 3K9.

This is a work of fiction. Names, characters, places and incidents are either the product of the author's imagination or are used fictitiously, and any resemblance to actual persons, living or dead, business establishments, events or locales is entirely coincidental.

This edition published by arrangement with Harlequin Books S.A.

® and TM are trademarks of the publisher. Trademarks indicated with ® are registered in the United States Patent and Trademark Office, the Canadian Trade Marks Office and in other countries.

www.eHarlequin.com

Printed in U.S.A.

Rebecca Winters, whose family of four children has now swelled to include three beautiful grandchildren, lives in Salt Lake City, Utah, in the land of the Rocky Mountains. With canyons and high Alpine meadows full of wildflowers, she never runs out of places to explore. They, plus her favorite vacation spots in Europe, often end up as backgrounds for her Harlequin Romance® novels, because writing is her passion, along with her family and church. Rebecca loves to hear from her readers. If you wish to e-mail her, please visit her Web site at www.rebeccawinters-author.com

Be swept away to Greece in Rebecca's next book:

The Lazaridis Marriage

In a tumbledown Greek farmhouse
working the land from dawn till dusk,
Greek tycoon Nikos Lazaridis tests heiress party-
girl Tracey Von Axel's resolve at every opportunity.
But as the sun sets over the fields, Nikos begins to
find it's his own resolve that's being tested....

Coming in July to Harlequin Romance®!

CHAPTER ONE

"Since the last two major college riots, we have to take what happened today seriously, Alex. I'm urging you to move yourself and your loved ones to one of your residences in the mountains away from the public where you're not so vulnerable."

"We've been over this ground before, Leo. I refuse to let fear rule our lives."

"Then at least consider permanently closing off public access to the castle and estate. There are too many radical student elements out there wanting to bring down the monarchy. They never stop thinking up new and ingenious ways to wreak havoc for the sheer hell of it."

"I agree there have always been those fringe elements in society, but I'd rather employ more security than shut myself off from the people."

In Alex's six years as king of the Romanche-speaking Valleder Canton in Switzerland, Leo had kept everyone safe, freeing Alex to attempt to do the job his father had done so superbly over a thirty-year period as sovereign.

He eyed Leo, the forty-year-old widower who'd been Interpol's top agent before becoming Alex's head of state security. They'd grown to be close friends.

"Tell me what happened."

"An extremely attractive American woman came through on the 10:00 a.m. tour of the castle. After it was over she told the guide she had business with you and asked that she be given an audience on a private matter. When told you didn't meet with the public she said, 'Not even if I have something of value to return to him?'

"Naturally the guide called for security. They brought her by police car to the downtown office. During my interrogation she said she had a ring of yours and knew you would want it back."

"A ring?"

Alex shook his head. "Where do these crazies come from? The only ring I have is the one my father gave me prior to his death six years ago. You're looking at it."

Leo folded his arms. "It's obvious the woman intentionally created a scene to see what would happen, and of course she got her wish.

"She was searched and her passport seized. When I asked to see the ring, she said she hadn't brought it with her because it was too valuable. But she had photos of it in the purse we confiscated."

A sound of incredulity escaped Alex's lips.

"This woman knew she would be detained and questioned. I'm positive she wanted to see how our security system works at the castle. Since the last demonstrators' attempt to storm the north gate, it isn't out of the realm of possibility they're hatching another plan to get the whole canton's attention and stir up trouble. Frankly I don't like it. Especially with your wedding only three weeks away."

"I don't like it, either," Alex admitted in a grim tone. If any of those incidents had hurt one of his family, he'd never forgive himself for not taking greater precautions. Thankfully Leo had been on top of things.

"What do you know about her?"

"She's a resident of Aurora, Colorado, named Darrell Collier."

Colorado?

Alex had been there, but he'd also been to several of the states in the U.S., even lived for a short period in Arizona.

"The woman is traveling alone under a newly issued American passport. She's never applied for one before. Her nonstop flight to Zurich originated in Denver, Colorado, yesterday morning.

"When she deplaned, the douanier asked her the reason for her visit. She said she was taking a short vacation. She rented a car and drove here last night where she stayed at the Hotel Otter. This morning she showed up for the tour.

"I checked her employment. She works for Gold Jet Airlines in the States making reservations. There's no police record on her, no outstanding warrants for her arrest in the U.S.

"I suppose she could be someone with a mental condition who stopped taking her medication. But my gut is telling me she's very much in her right mind and working for some anti-royal group trying to discover the castle's vulnerabilities.

"How many tourists traveling alone go straight from the plane to one castle for a short visit? It just doesn't add up. So far she's been calm and cooperative. She's one cool customer."

"In other words she's willing to sacrifice herself for information," Alex muttered.

The other man cast him a shrewd regard. "She hasn't committed a crime and knew we had to release her. She's been escorted back to the airport in Zurich. I've already alerted the American authorities. Once her flight leaves for the States, they'll keep tabs on her. It's the best we can do about her for now. My main concern is you and your family."

That was twice in few minutes he'd talked about Alex's family. Leo had more than a passing interest in Alex's cousin-in-law Evelyn who lived on the estate and had lost her husband. Nothing would please him more than to see the two of them get together. But since Evelyn was a royal, Leo would never dare to presume.

"Greater measures need to be taken to protect all of you," Leo emphasized again.

Alex decided to help things along. "Let's double the security on the whole estate. It wouldn't hurt if you went along with Evelyn the next time she goes riding or shopping. Warn her and the boys to be extra careful. Coming from you personally, she'll take it better than from me."

"I'll be happy to do that," he answered in a calm voice, but Alex saw the flare of excitement in his eyes. "This is a start in the right direction. I'll take care of it immediately."

As he stood up, he put an eight by ten envelope on the desk in front of Alex. "These are enlarged copies of the colored photos of the ring which could have been purchased in any of the canton's souvenir shops. There's an inscription on the band in Romanche, but the sentiment doesn't send up any red flags. My men are tracking down the regional jeweler as we speak.

"Like I said, she came to the castle with a definite agenda."

After he left the room, Alex reached for the envelope whose contents served as a reminder of his official engagement to Isabella. It wouldn't be long before he was a married man. He hadn't been able to put it off any longer. If it had been up to Isabella, they'd have said their vows several years earlier.

His alliance with the princess of San Ravino, Italy, would cement certain lucrative business relationships Alex's father had instigated with the king of San Ravino when Alex had been in his mid-teens.

On his father's death bed he'd said, "A king needs a wife, Alex, and your mother needs a grandchild. Isabella is an intelligent, beautiful woman and will give you children you can be proud of."

Admittedly Isabella with her black hair turned heads. Nine years younger than Alex, she would be biddable and make the perfect consort. Alex agreed the princess had qualities he admired. There'd be no surprises. Everyone was excited for the wedding. Everyone except him...

With a jerking motion he upended the envelope. Out spilled four photos of a man's gold ring taken at different angles.

As Leo had said, the colorful enamel work showing the Valleder coat of arms appeared on pins, rings, virtually any piece of jewelry a tourist could take home as a reminder of their trip to the heart of the Swiss Alps.

The last photograph revealed the inscription on the inner band in the Puter dialect. Alex looked closer.

More than a cousin.

He closed his eyes tightly in pain.

This was the ring his deceased cousin, Chaz, had given him on his sixteenth birthday—the same ring he'd somehow parted with during a certain vacation to Colorado when he and Chaz had turned twenty. On that trip his cousin had urged him to forget he was a royal and simply live it up like they were two ordinary guys.

Alex sprang from his swivel chair, hardly able to comprehend that the young woman he'd given it to under fuzzy circumstances could be the woman who'd come to the castle trying to arrange a meeting with him.

These photos were the proof that something of significance had happened on that trip. He didn't like what he was thinking, especially when his recollection of those events was a blur. This had to be an extortion tactic.

With no time to lose he pressed the programmed digit on his cell phone. It was his private line to Leo.

"Yes, Alex?"

"You've more than earned your pay today, my friend."

"What do you mean? What's going on?"

Alex wished he knew. "It's my ring, Leo. One I parted with a long time ago, but the memory is hazy." Since that experience he'd done everything in his power to be a good king, including agreeing to marry the princess his parents favored. No hint of scandal had touched his life until now, less than a month before his wedding...

"When exactly?" the other man fired.

"Thirteen years ago while I was on a trip, Chaz and I spent a wild night drinking with some girls. Things got out of control. I'd forgotten until I saw the photos."

Leo let out a low whistle. "That doesn't sound like you."

"Don't be fooled. I have a few skeletons lying around."

His friend made a strange sound in his throat. "This one might have come back to bite you, if you follow my meaning."

"I know exactly what you mean."

Depending on this woman's agenda, she could hurt him and the people he loved in ways he refused to let happen.

There was a palpable silence, then Leo asked, "How can I help? I've done everything to keep this suppressed, but you never know."

"Tell me about it," he muttered. "I'm going on a private fishing expedition, Leo. Alert your most trusted men to board my jet within the hour. The second this woman's flight leaves the ground, I want to be notified."

"Consider it done." After another silence, "Alex—"

"I know what you're going to say, Leo. But I'm afraid the time for damage control was years ago."

By the time Darrell Collier's jet landed at the Denver airport, she'd cried all the tears she was going to cry. Her final, foolhardy attempt to unite her adopted son with his phantom father had completely failed. To her deep-felt sorrow, Phillip would never know the name or the whereabouts of the man who'd impregnated Darrell's sister before disappearing from her life.

Deprived of the father he'd never known, Phillip was entering his teens with a giant chip on his shoulder.

Darrell loved him with her whole heart and soul, but his anger at fate had made him so difficult to handle these days, she realized she needed to get professional help for him.

Things were building to a crisis state. She felt more helpless now than when Melissa had died after giving birth twelve years ago, leaving Darrell to raise her sweet little dark-blond boy alone.

It had been the two of them against the world.

After her final effort to make contact with his father, it was still the two of them forging ahead alone. That was the way it would always be.

She could only hope that in time he would let the anger go and embrace his life. He had everything to live for, but right now he couldn't see beyond the unfairness of an existence without a dad. Emotionally he reminded her of Melissa, who'd also felt deprived because of a car accident that had robbed them of their parents.

Her pain had turned her into a willful and tempestuous teen their grandmother couldn't handle. It appeared history would be repeating itself unless Darrell took an active stance to help Phillip before it was too late.

Having a plan was better than no plan, she told herself as she took the train to get her luggage. After retrieving it, she left the terminal and headed for the parking lot, anxious to get home. She'd been gone three days and missed him horribly. She couldn't wait to pick him up.

Eventually she reached her compact car. As she was putting

her suitcase in the trunk, two men suddenly appeared out of nowhere dressed in shirt sleeves and Jamaica shorts.

"Ms. Collier?"

Though it was midafternoon and there were other people around, she suddenly felt nervous. "Yes?"

They flashed her their photo ID cards.

FBI?

"If you'll come with us, we'll take you to a place where you can meet with the king of Valleder in private."

Darrell was convinced she was hallucinating. After the balmy temperatures in Switzerland, this long walk in the sweltering one hundred degree July heat must have gotten to her.

"The king is *here?* In *Denver?*"

"Yes, ma'am. He's made it possible for you to discuss a certain private matter with him."

The other federal agent handed her the envelope containing the photos she'd left with the police in the capital city of Bris.

So he *had* recognized the ring.

After giving up all hope, she was incredulous this was happening now. In a daze she slowly shut the trunk lid.

"The king is waiting. We'll bring you back to your car later."

The next few minutes passed in a blur as she was helped into the back seat of an unmarked car. One of the agents sat next to her. The other sat in front next to the driver. At a glance she realized there were several unmarked cars with agents forming a cortege.

The driver left the airport and took the E470, a toll road that eventually led to the Centennial Airport where the private jets landed. They wound around to a gleaming white jet with the Valleder royal coat of arms on the side.

She saw the stairs being lowered. Security people were everywhere.

One of them greeted her after she'd gotten out of the car. Another stood at the bottom of the stairs.

"His Majesty is just inside. Go ahead."

Feeling she was in some sort of trance, Darrell climbed the steps, wondering if she'd wake up before she reached the opening.

"Oh—" she cried softly when a well honed male who stood six foot three stepped out from the interior.

He was a stranger, yet because of certain physical traits that reminded her of Phillip, he looked familiar, too.

A relentless afternoon sun gilded the natural highlights of his wavy dark-blond hair.

The Internet pictures of the king of Valleder could never do justice to his rugged masculine appeal, let alone capture the intensity of his unique hazel eyes.

His gaze traveled over her classic features that hadn't seen makeup in twelve hours. It lingered on her puffy, tear-swollen eyes the color of drenched pansies. With her shoulder-length ash-blond hair needing a shampoo, and her aqua blouse and skirt looking less than fresh, she'd never felt a bigger mess.

The realization that she was standing before the king she'd risked a great deal to meet was so surreal, she couldn't think clearly.

He had her at a distinct disadvantage. As his gaze swept over her feminine attributes, heat rose through her body from her curling toes to the crown of her head.

Compelled by a force stronger than her will, her gaze took in his white sport shirt covering a well-defined chest. He wore tan chinos that molded his rock-hard legs, hinting at powerful thighs.

Looking at him made her realize that one day her tall, lanky son would resemble his attractive father in quite a few ways.

"Ms. Collier, I presume?"

Still in disbelief that he'd flown all this way, she was too tongue-tied to think with any coherence. She cleared her throat. "Yes. I know you're the king, but I—I don't know what to call you," she stammered in embarrassment.

"I realize the situation is foreign to you. Under the circumstances just call me Alex. It appears we have something important to discuss. Please come in." He spoke impeccable English with virtually no trace of accent.

Once over the threshold, she entered a world where only the privileged conducted business thousands of miles above the earth. Besides everything else, the air-conditioning was heavenly.

He led her to a room with a grouping of furniture much like an elegant den. The second she sat down on one of the couches, a steward appeared with a tray of drinks. She chose cola, then sat on the edge of the luxurious white upholstery unable to relax. Again she had the feeling she was existing in another state of consciousness.

He took a chair opposite her, the picture of urbane sophistication while he drank coffee.

"Why don't we start by you telling me how you came by that ring."

He'd come straight to the point, not appearing worried about the history behind it.

Her heart pounded so hard she was certain he could hear it in the confines of the room.

"My sister entrusted it to me."

He put the coffee cup on a side table and leaned forward. "What's her name?"

How strange to be talking about her sister, the woman he'd enamored to the point she would have done anything for him, and did.

"Melissa Collier. Does that mean anything to you?"

He eyed her with an enigmatic expression. "I'm sorry to say it doesn't."

His response came as no surprise to Darrell. After thirteen years, how many men in his position remembered the names of the girls they'd been with for a one-night stand? Particularly a rebellious yet vulnerable teen like Melissa. She'd probably made up a fake name so she wouldn't get into trouble with the management where she worked.

He rubbed his lower lip with his thumb, mesmerizing Darrell. "Why didn't she come to Bris?"

Darrell drew in a shaky breath. "Because she died twelve years ago."

Lines darkened his striking features. "I'm sorry," he whispered, sounding surprisingly sincere.

"So am I." Her voice faltered.

"How did she die?"

There's your opening, Darrell.

Yet oddly enough she found herself unable to go on. No matter how long she'd prayed for this moment for Phillip's sake, what the king was about to hear was going to change his life. She found she couldn't do this to him. The shock would be too enormous to any man, let alone a king— What had she been thinking?

"It doesn't really matter. All I know is, she wanted you to have the ring back because she knew it was valuable."

"The ring has gotten my attention. Now I want to know what's behind it."

Darrell felt ill. "I—I made a mistake coming to Switzerland. Haven't you ever made one?" she cried in panic. "Let me just get the ring for you and then you can go home and we'll forget this ever happened. Please—"

"I'm afraid I can't do that."

Tears ran down her face. "I don't want to hurt you. I don't want *anyone* to be hurt—"

She had to get out of there, but before she reached the doorway, he said, "The best way to hurt me is to make a scene in front of my staff. Why don't you sit down and answer my question about your sister."

Realizing he wouldn't go away until he knew the truth, Darrell wiped her eyes and finally did his bidding.

"Two days after she gave birth to an eight-pound boy, a brain aneurism took her life."

A pulsating silence filled the cabin.

His body didn't move, but she saw a flicker in the depths of his eyes, turning them the green of a stormy ocean.

"Do you have pictures of them on you?"

She'd thought he'd deny it was his son, or at least question her outrageous suggestion that he might have been the father.

He did neither. Instead he'd responded in a forthright manner that astounded her.

"I have a packet in my wallet. The photo of Melissa is her junior year high school picture. The rest are pictures of my son taken on every birthday in case I ever found his father and he wanted to see them."

One dark brow lifted. "Your son?"

"Yes. I adopted him."

"You never married?"

"No."

Her hands trembled as she opened her purse and pulled the packet from her wallet.

He got up and reached for it.

She held her breath while he stood there with his legs slightly apart, studying each photograph with an intensity that held her spellbound.

The likeness of his son to him couldn't be disputed.

"What day was he born?"

"February 27. He'll be thirteen on his next birthday."

He examined the pictures for a long time. "What did you name him?" His voice revealed a husky quality that indicated he was deeply moved. Another surprise.

"When Melissa had an ultrasound and found out she was going to have a boy, she named him after you."

His gaze shot to hers. "I have several names."

Darrell's mouth had gone dry. "I know. I saw the long list on the Internet. You told her you were Phil from New York. So Melissa called him Phillip."

A haunted expression crossed over his features, making the thirty-three-year-old monarch appear older than he was.

"Now that I see her picture, I do remember visiting a dude ranch in Colorado Springs in June thirteen years ago. A college girl a little shorter than you with hair several shades darker than yours worked there."

"Yes. That was Melissa. She was a room maid for the summer. Except that she wasn't in college. She was only seventeen, and had another year of high school ahead of her."

His lips thinned.

"Don't worry," Darrell murmured. "I'm sure she lied about her age. She looked older and couldn't grow up fast enough. She said you'd both been drinking and got into a sleeping bag under the stars. That's when you parted with the ring.

"Knowing Melissa, she probably begged you to let her put it on. Especially after you told her you were really a prince.

"I thought the whole story was bogus. But two weeks ago when I consulted a heraldry expert who identified your family's coat of arms, I had to take it seriously.

"The Internet articles and pictures of you helped me with the rest. Not only was one of your names Phillip, I read that you were the prince of Bris before your coronation six years ago. Suddenly everything fell into place. But like all fairy tales, her glorious interlude with you came to a bitter end.

"When she reported for work the next day, you'd already disappeared without a trace. All she had of you was the ring. Before she died, she begged me to find you. After the funeral, I hid it away."

His jaw hardened. Darrell could feel the tension emanating from him.

"How you must despise me." His deep voice throbbed with self-abnegation. "Under the circumstances, why didn't you tell the police what you've just told me? It was the perfect opportunity to expose me."

Though she didn't want to feel any compassion for him, there was something innately honorable about him owning up to his past behavior without offering excuses.

She hadn't expected it of him. She hadn't expected to have a positive feeling anywhere in her body for this man who'd made her sister pregnant, indirectly bringing on her early death.

Darrell rubbed her eyes with her palms.

"The last thing on my mind was creating a scandal for you. What happened between you and Melissa has happened to millions of couples since time immemorial. The difference is, not every child turns out to be the son of a king.

"Phillip wants his father more than you can imagine. Lately he's been angry over the fact that you're out in the cosmos someplace, unaware he's alive. He's wishing with all his heart and soul that he had a dad like his friends. He's become quite inconsolable.

"But now that I've found you, I realize it was a mistake. I had no right to disrupt your life even if my son is suffering. He wouldn't be the only child in the world to grow up without a father.

"The problem is, after raising him from birth I love him

too much. The saying about a mother rushing into a burning building to save her child is truer than even *I* knew until now."

She lifted her head and stared up at him with glistening eyes. "In this life there are some things that happen which are better left alone. This is one of them."

"How can you say that?" he asked in a low voice. "I'm responsible for her pregnancy. I wish I'd known of Phillip's existence from the beginning."

"It would only have complicated your life. While I was checking out of the Hotel Otter, I overheard the desk clerk telling a tourist that there's going to be a royal wedding at the end of July. I heard him say you were marrying a princess named Isabella.

"Learning you've been betrothed for several years, that news made me glad I hadn't been able to talk to you. Please be assured neither you nor your intended bride will ever see or hear from me again."

Alex moved as if to speak but Darrell rushed on, not giving him the chance to interrupt her. "If you'll wait before flying back to Bris, I'll drive home and ask one of the agents to bring the ring to you."

She jumped to her feet, "Forgive me for forcing you to fly all this way. I'm so sorry—" she whispered before rushing out of the cabin and down the stairs of the jet.

"Please take me to my car, then follow me home. I have something of the king's you need to return to him before he leaves the airport."

The agent looked surprised, but he helped her in the car and instructed the man at the wheel to go back to the main airport's parking lot.

A half hour later Darrell was still trembling as she pulled into the driveway of her small, two-bedroom condo. The agent's car pulled in behind her.

She dashed in the house and hurried up the stairs to her closet. The ring was inside a little velvet pouch she kept in the pocket of an ancient winter coat she'd never thrown out.

Within seconds she'd run back outside and handed it to him through the car window. He nodded to her before they drove off, taking all incriminating evidence with them. Only then did she realize the king still had the pictures of Melissa and Phillip.

That was all right. Whatever he did with them, it didn't matter. She had duplicates.

So…it was over. Phillip's father would remain Phil from New York. End of story.

The pilot buzzed Alex. "Your Majesty? We're ready for takeoff at anytime."

Alex's hand closed around the ring the agent had brought to him moments ago. "Thank you. I'll get back to you in a minute."

He'd laid out Darrell Collier's photos on the desk in front of him. As he studied each one, his father's voice seemed to call out from the grave. "Always remember that one day you'll be King."

One wild night thirteen years ago he'd rebelled against the rules governing his royal life with *this* the result.

He actually had a son from his own body named Phillip.

Alex was a father!

Dear Lord—how could he just fly back to Switzerland as if nothing had happened, his secret safely hidden forever?

Maybe an ambitious king with no soul, or an unscrupulous man with no moral conscience, was capable of it. Ms. Collier had made a promise he would never hear from her again, that Phillip would never learn his father's identity. Alex believed her.

But he knew himself too well. There was no way he could turn his back on his own flesh and blood no matter how the reality would impact his personal or political life. The knowledge that he had a son living in Denver, Colorado, would eat him alive.

Phillip hadn't asked to be born.

He was the innocent product of an irresponsible twenty-year-old and an underage teen! By some miracle Darrell Collier had been there to mother Phillip and do the job Alex should have been doing all along.

Twelve years without a father.

Alex couldn't imagine it, not when his own father had been such a dominant force in his life.

Without hesitation he buzzed his pilot. "I'm not leaving Denver yet. Stand by. I'll get back to you as soon as I know my plans."

He then rang the agent who'd brought him the ring. "Get everyone ready. I have a visit to make to Ms. Collier's home."

After a strange silence, "Yes, Your Majesty."

CHAPTER TWO

DARRELL got in her car and drove over to the Holbrooks's to pick up Phillip. En route she phoned to tell him she was on her way.

It was ten to six in the evening when she pulled up in front and honked. Phillip was waiting for her, and came out the door with his sleeping and duffel bags.

Hugs from him had been on short ration over the last year, but he actually gave her one after getting in the car. It melted her heart.

She'd been away three days, the longest separation they'd ever had. Over the years the two of them had enjoyed her airline perks. They'd gone on many vacations to fun places around the U.S. and Hawaii. But the trip to Bris had been for her eyes only, which meant Phillip had to stay with his best friend. Many weekends she'd let Ryan sleep over at her condo while his parents were out of town.

"How did it go while I was away?"

"Okay."

"Tell me about the swim meet."

"I didn't place."

Then he didn't try hard enough because he usually took more firsts than the other guys on the team!

"Oh well, There's always next time."

"How come you didn't take me to Chicago with you?"

She drew in a deep breath. "I couldn't. It was an exhausting business trip. But I have an idea. After we get back to the condo and I freshen up, how would you like to go somewhere for dinner? You name the place."

"Why do we have to go out? Can't we just stay home?"

To her disappointment, he was more truculent than usual. She reached out to squeeze his arm. "Sure we can. I'll fix us some tacos and we'll just hang out."

When he didn't respond she said, "I don't know if I told you Danice was transferred to Washington D.C. She's invited us to spend the Fourth of July with her. That's the day after tomorrow. We'll watch the fireworks from a boat on the Potomac. It'll be fabulous. What do you say?"

"I'd rather not go."

Darrell moaned inwardly. "How come?"

"Danice treats me like a little kid. I hate it."

Danice was her good friend, but right now Phillip didn't care how he sounded. She started to feel panicky. His depression was definitely worse.

"Here we are," she said unnecessarily as she pulled into the garage of their condo. "Take your clothes into the laundry room and we'll get a wash started."

"Mrs. Holbrook already did mine."

"That was nice of her."

When Darrell reached for her suitcase and saw the Zurich tag on the handle, she tore it off and stuffed it in her purse before entering the hallway.

She was convinced he was suffering more than usual because he'd just come from Ryan's, whose father was known as Mr. Dad.

Phillip only had a mom. Life was unfair.

It *was* unfair.

Darrell no longer had a sibling. With her grandmother already passed away, Darrell had been virtually alone when she'd taken on the role of mother to raise Phillip.

Over the years she'd dated off and on. She'd even come close to marrying her boss earlier this year. But he was too soft on Phillip who needed a strong hand. Darrell had feared her son would always be in the driver's seat after they married, so she'd stopped seeing him except in connection with her work.

Since then she hadn't dated anyone.

"Phillip?" she called to him. "I'll be upstairs changing, then I'll come down and fix us a meal."

"Okay."

The condo felt like an oven. On the way up to the bathroom she turned on the air-conditioning to cool off the house.

Once beneath the spray, she quickly lathered her hair, then used the blow dryer until the strands swished soft and silky against her shoulders.

Afraid to keep him waiting too long, she applied a fresh coat of coral frost lipstick, then slipped on white shorts and a sleeveless navy top. Dispensing with shoes she hurried downstairs. He needed to talk.

She knew the drill. They would discuss all sorts of things, but inevitably he'd bring the conversation around to the father he was growing to hate for not being there for him.

It was so sad he'd reached the age where he understood about a man sowing his wild oats without compunction, and one had taken root in the Rocky Mountains.

Heartsick for Phillip who was acting out with increased frequency, she walked in the family room off the kitchen to find him. He was playing a video game. In her opinion they were a curse. No communication could go on with his hands on the controls, and his eyes glued to the screen. Luckily he enjoyed sports, which kept him busy a lot of the time now that it was summer.

"Want to grate the cheese and cut up the tomatoes?"

Without saying anything he got up and followed her to the fridge. Athletically inclined, he looked good in his old cutoffs and T-shirt. One day he would look…fantastic, just like his father, whose arresting features and physique eclipsed those of any man she'd ever known.

She could still picture him standing in the doorway of the jet, staring at her with those hauntingly beautiful green-gray eyes. They seemed to follow her into the kitchen where she fried the tortillas and ground beef. Then she and Phillip sat down to eat.

She was glad to see his dark mood hadn't affected his appetite. She waited until he'd finished off his third taco before venturing into uncharted waters.

"Sweetheart?" she began. "I love you more than you'll ever know, and it hurts me that you're so unhappy. There's an old adage that says something like, 'Give me the wisdom to accept the things I can't change, and help me to change the things I need to do something about.' It's a good rule to live by.

"No matter how much you want things to be different, your father didn't stay in Colorado, so he didn't know you were born. That's the painful fact of the matter.

"Now the ball is in your court. You can either make up your mind it's not going to ruin your life, or you can grow up an angry man so fixated on your own hurt, you'll never live up to your full potential.

"I know I'm just your dumb mom, but between us, we're all we've got. I promised your mother I'd love you and take care of you forever. So I think the time has come for you to go to a counselor you can talk to. Someone impartial who will listen to whatever you feel like saying and won't judge you."

"No way—" He flung himself out of the chair. His blue-gray eyes glittered with unshed tears. "I'm not crazy!"

"Of course not, but you *are* in pain and a counselor might be able to help you where I can't."

His expression stiffened. "I won't go to a shrink and you can't make me!"

The next thing she knew, the front door slammed.

Darrell sat there in shock. Just before he'd bolted, he'd looked and sounded exactly like Melissa.

With her heart aching, she ran over to the sink to look out the window. He was already halfway down the street on his dirt bike. He'd never exploded like this before. She had to go after him. Grabbing her purse, she hurried into the garage and backed the car out.

She doubted he had a destination in mind. All she could do was drive in the direction he'd gone. But after ten minutes of searching the neighborhood for him, she realized he intended to stay lost for a while.

Defeated, she drove back to the condo and made a call to a couple of his friends. Eventually she found out from Steve's stepmom he'd gone swimming. They'd probably be back in an hour.

Relief swept through Darrell. Hopefully he would come home a little less angry and they'd be able to start over.

While she cleaned up the kitchen, she heard the doorbell ring.

He must have come back to get his swimming suit and had forgotten his key.

She hurried to unlock the door.

"Phillip sweetheart?" she cried as she flung it open, prepared to give him a hug whether he wanted one or not.

But instead of a belligerent twelve-year-old boy standing

there on the porch, a solidly built male filled the aperture. A man she'd presumed was already in the air on his way back to Switzerland.

Beyond his broad shoulder she glimpsed a bulletproof limo with smoked glass parked in front. She didn't doubt for a second his security people had surrounded the complex where she lived, providing heavy protection for him.

"Hello again, Darrell Collier. In case you've forgotten, my name is Alex." His deep male voice resonated to her insides.

Speechless and feeling light-headed, she held on to the door for support. "I—I'm sorry, Alex." She stumbled over her words. "But I never expected to see you again."

He studied her upturned features for a moment. "You made that abundantly clear when you flew out of my cabin a little while ago."

Her heart thundered in her chest. "Didn't you get the ring?"

His eyes glinted with a mysterious light. "It's in my pocket."

"Then I don't understand. If you're here to give me hush money or some such thing, I wouldn't take it. I swear before God I could never do that to you or anyone else."

He said nothing.

She shook her head, causing her hair to swirl a silvery-gold. "You shouldn't have come," she said in a shaky voice. "Phillip will be home soon and see the limo. If he finds you here, he'll ask questions and it won't take him long to notice certain…similarities."

Her unexpected visitor straightened to his full, intimidating height. "Then I guess I'll have to take that chance because you and I still have things to discuss. May I come in?"

She couldn't sustain his penetrating glance and averted her eyes. "I—I don't think that's a good idea."

"I happen to disagree with you," he came back with a

strong hint of authority in his voice. "If you prefer, we can sit in the limo."

"No—" she blurted. With her bare legs showing and no shoes on her feet, the thought of being confined with him sounded far too intimate.

"Are you going to make a grown king beg? It's a position I don't recall having been in before."

Everything he said and did was getting under her skin, confusing and exciting her when she shouldn't be having any feelings at all!

She moistened her lips nervously. "I didn't mean to be rude. Please— Come in."

"Since you put it so nicely, I think I will."

His male mouth twitched, revealing a charm that was lethal. No wonder Melissa had fallen for him. Of course he'd only been twenty or so at the time, but it wouldn't have made any difference. Some men were just endowed at an early age with a raw, virile charisma few women could resist.

When Melissa had talked about lying in his arms beneath the stars, Darrell had absorbed the revelation on an intellectual level. To see her sister's lover in the flesh was like coming too close to a solar flare that scorched the body and filled her with a strange envy.

Melissa may have only been a teenager, but she'd known rapture with this exciting man who ruled a kingdom. She'd carried his son to term. Those joys were something Darrell had yet to experience for herself, if she ever did.

Her front door opened into the small living room with its traditional decor. His presence dwarfed the interior.

"Make yourself comfortable. I'll be right back."

She felt his appraising gaze on her legs as she darted up the stairs. By the time she returned wearing a pair of pleated white sailor pants and leather sandals, she felt a little more presentable.

Darrell found him studying some framed family pictures. He appeared deep in thought.

When he heard her enter, he put down the picture of Phillip and turned in her direction. His eyes roved over her trembling figure, silently acknowledging the change in her attire.

"By the way you answered the door just now, I take it you haven't seen Phillip since you arrived back."

She smoothed her damp palms against her hips, a gesture he also noted. "Actually I have. But while we were eating dinner, I said something that upset him. He flew out the door and went off on his bike. I was hoping he'd decided to come back."

He frowned. "You seemed unduly anxious. Does he often blow up like that?"

Already he was sounding like a concerned parent. She hardly knew what to make of this remarkably handsome stranger from another continent.

"I said something that frightened him."

"What was that?" her guest persisted.

"The three days away from him let me see how depressed he has become. I told him I was going to take him to a counselor to help him deal with his issues of abandonment. He yelled that he wasn't crazy before he charged out of here like a torpedo."

She rubbed her arms with her hands. "On the flight home from Switzerland, I made up my mind I wasn't going to wait any longer to get help for him. I knew he would fight me on this, but I'm committed. In all honesty, I should have taken him to a doctor long before now. He's showing the same pattern Melissa did."

He moved closer, his gaze intent on her face. "Tell me about your family."

"My parents met at Denver University. Mother would have been a teacher. Dad was studying to become a geologist. Melissa had barely turned two when they were killed in a car accident and my grandmother Alice took on the responsibility of raising us.

"She was a wonderful person. We both adored her, but Melissa had a harder time of it. She yearned for our parents even though she didn't remember them. As she got older, she felt more and more sorry for herself. In time she grew petulant like Phillip and became too much of a handful for Grandma whose health began to fail.

"When Melissa had an opportunity to work at the dude ranch through a close friend's family, she didn't hesitate. She knew a lot of famous VIPs vacationed there. She'd made up her mind she was going to meet an important man who would take her away and give her the kind of life that would make up for her deprivation."

His eyes studied her intently. "What about you? A teenager burdened with sorrow and a new baby to raise. How did you do it all?"

"Grandma's house was paid for. I took a night job I could do at home for the airlines making reservations. Eventually I was able to start taking college classes and graduated in communications.

"The company gave me a promotion, so I sold the house and bought this condo, which is closer to my work. Everything seemed fine, but it wasn't fine to Phillip."

Darrell's eyes filled with liquid. "It's a tragic irony Melissa met *you,* a *real* prince. There's a lesson to be learned here in getting what you wish for…" Her voice trailed.

He trapped her gaze. "I can't do anything about your sister now, but it's not too late for Phillip."

Her thoughts reeled. "It is where *you're* concerned," she said in a dull voice.

She heard his sharp intake of breath. "He's my son. It's high time we got to know each other."

"You don't really mean that. You couldn't—" she cried. "It will change your whole life."

"That's what children do when they come into the world. He's a precious gift."

"But you're a king! This is going to complicate your life in ways I can't even begin to imagine, starting with salacious reports from the press."

"What else is new. I'm a man first, Darrell. When I fathered Phillip, I wasn't yet a king. I've already missed the first twelve years of his life. As my mother keeps telling me, a grandmother needs grandchildren. After she gets over the shock, she's going to be thrilled."

Darrell was afraid to believe him. But when she looked deeper into his eyes, she knew instinctively he believed what he was saying.

She swallowed hard. "You haven't even met him yet. He's very complex."

"You mean he's damned difficult most of the time, but sweet as honey at unexpected moments?"

"That's exactly how he is," her voice shook.

He put his hands on his hips in a wholly male stance. "He's a Valleder all right. Our genes don't lie. After we meet, he might never grow to like me, but we share the same blood. That makes us family, sight unseen."

Darrell hugged her arms to her waist. "What about your marriage? Phillip's existence is going to come as a huge shock to the woman you've chosen. It isn't fair to her."

His eyes held a faraway look. "The news that I have a son is going to turn the entire canton on its ear. However I'm not particularly concerned about anyone but Phillip. You've had the whole responsibility of him all this time. Now it's my turn."

She bit her lower lip. "It'll transform him to know he has a father he can talk to on the phone sometimes."

His expression sobered. "I hope so, but first we have to get over the biggest hurdle. He has viewed me as a deadbeat dad for a lot of years. I have a feeling this is going to take some time."

He checked his watch. "It's starting to get dark. Where do you think he could be?"

"I called some of his friends. They went swimming at the condo pool."

"Why don't we drive over in your car and find him. I'll tell him I'm an old friend of his mother's and we'll go from there."

Her heart raced too fast. "I don't know, Alex. Maybe you'd better think about this for a while longer. Once the water spills over the dam…"

A shadow crossed his face. "Isn't this why you came to Bris?"

"Yes. But when I found out you're going to be married soon, I was glad I'd been prevented from meeting you.

"My grandmother died when Phillip was nine months old. She urged me to adopt him. She also told me not to go looking for you unless I was prepared to deal with the consequences. Until Phillip became so difficult, I'd made up my mind to follow her advice.

His eyes narrowed on her face. "I don't know of another woman whose love for a child she didn't give birth to would cause her to put everything on the line to make him happy.

"For you to sacrifice your own life for him tells me all I need to know about your character. My son has been more fortunate than he'll ever know," his voice grated. "I owe you a debt of gratitude I'll never be able to repay for what you've done, Darrell."

"It's been no sacrifice—he was the most adorable baby on this earth. I fell in love with him on sight. He's my life!"

"To know I have a son makes me feel the same way," he asserted in a solemn tone. "So why don't you make that phone call. After seeing his pictures, I'm eager to lay eyes on him in person."

She felt that eagerness. It wasn't an emotion he could feign. Nervous excitement welled up inside her. "All right. The phone's in the other room."

He followed her to the family room. As she picked up the wall phone receiver in the kitchen and started to press the digits, they both heard the front door open.

"Mom? What's that black limo doing outside our house? Doug saw it on his way over to the pool and told me."

Her anxious glance darted to Alex before she hung up the phone. In the next instant Phillip appeared in the family room. His hair was still damp from his swim. It looked darker when it was wet.

Melissa had been a beautiful girl with a ton of boyfriends. Darrell had always thought her son was the best looking boy out of all his friends. He seemed older than most of the seventh-graders and was growing more attractive all the time. Talk about the acorn falling close to the mighty oak—

But Darrell received an unexpected jolt when Phillip took one glance at Alex and went pale with fright. She recognized that look. What on earth?

His gaze switched to Darrell. "Is this that counselor you were talking about?"

Aghast, she said, "No, sweetheart. No— This man—" She struggled. "This man—"

"What your mother is trying to say is that I'm Phil."

With those words, Darrell felt a strange charge in the atmosphere followed by a stillness that fell over Phillip.

He studied Alex for such a long time, Darrell wondered if he'd slipped into some kind of catatonic state.

"You're my dad," he finally muttered because he could see part of himself in the imposing stranger whose candor took Darrell's breath.

"I'm sorry it has taken us so long to meet."

Phillip's body started to tremble in reaction. His eyes filled. "I hate you."

"Phillip—" Darrel was horrified.

"I don't blame you," Alex responded with a calm she could only envy.

"I'd hate me, too, if I were in your shoes. But there's something you need to know. My father's brother was in a serious boating accident while I was on vacation in Colorado Springs thirteen years ago with my cousin Chaz. The doctors weren't sure he was going to live.

"When we got the news, we flew straight home. Fortunately he pulled through. I would have come back to Colorado later, but my father had other plans for me. By the time I tried to reach your mother by phone, it was fall and she didn't work at the dude ranch anymore. For security reasons no one would give me any information about her. I'm afraid time and circumstances separated us through no fault of our own."

During Alex's explanation, Phillip's hands kept forming fists. Suddenly he dashed out of the room. Darrell heard him run up the stairs and slam his bedroom door.

She shook her head. "I can't believe he said that to you."

"After knowing what he's been thinking all these years, *I* can. In fact I would have been surprised if he'd said anything else."

"He's changed so much from the darling, funny boy who used to play jokes and tease."

She almost choked on her tears. "I—I'd better go up to him."

"Let's let him work this through on his own. He's just sustained an enormous shock and will come around when he's ready."

Alex had a lot more confidence in the situation than she did. Maybe it took a man's perspective in a crisis like this. Except that Alex wasn't just any man.

Darrell eyed him covertly. Though he hid it well, she knew

Phillip couldn't be the only one shaken. Alex had just come face-to-face with a son he didn't know he had until a few hours ago.

Her heart warmed to him because he'd given his son certain information to make him feel better about the circumstances surrounding his conception.

She'd seen Phillip's eyes flare in surprise at the unexpected explanation. It remained to be seen if he would accept what his father had told him.

At the crucial moment Alex had known exactly what to say to disarm him. It was the master stroke of a man who put out fires every day in his role as king.

She was still unable to credit that he was willing to risk the fallout from the public scandal this would create in order to be united with his son.

Even if he tried to keep the news quiet, it would come out. His sterling reputation as the ruler of the canton would be tainted.

The woman he was betrothed to would suffer anguish.

He talked about his mother being thrilled with the news once she heard she was already a grandmother. But that wasn't the way it was likely to work. His mother would not be thrilled or anything close to it!

Darrell was frightened for him.

Her anxiety must have shown on her face and in her body language because he said, "Relax, Darrell. I know what I'm doing. While we wait for him to reappear, how about feeding a starving man."

He wanted food at a time like this? But then she remembered that Phillip could always eat in a crisis. It was one telling example of the ties that bound this father to this son.

"I have tacos left over from dinner. I'll warm them up for you."

"Sounds delicious. What can I do to help?"

"There's instant coffee in that cupboard."

"I'll make it," he offered. "It's something I'm good at."

The man was good at so many things, Darrell was in danger of losing her perspective altogether.

They worked in harmony, then sat down at the table like two ordinary people. But there was nothing ordinary about this situation or him!

Terrified of what was going on upstairs, she sipped her coffee without tasting it.

Alex on the other hand seemed to devour the six tacos with relish. After drinking several cups of the steaming brew, he made a sound of satisfaction.

"The Valleder Canton is renowned for its excellent cuisine, but I have to tell you they don't serve anything this good."

The secret to not falling apart right now was to keep making small talk.

"Yes, they do. I had a fondue bourguignonne dinner to die for at the Hotel Otter. But I must admit authentic Mexican food is hard to come by outside the western part of the U.S."

When her cell phone rang, she jumped up from the table and hurried over to the counter to get it out of her purse. She checked the caller ID. It was Danice who no doubt was trying to make final plans for the Fourth.

Darrell couldn't talk right now. Later on tonight she'd return her call.

Alex took the dishes over to the sink. "If you want privacy to talk to the man you're involved with, I'll be happy to go in the living room,"

"I'm not involved with anyone right now, but thank you anyway."

He studied her briefly. "Being a good parent is a full-time job."

"For Phillip to say what he did to you doesn't make me sound like a good parent or anything close. I've never seen him that rude to anyone in my life."

She was about to ask Alex how he knew about the trials of

a parent when he said, "My cousin-in-law, Evelyn, is raising two boys on her own. They run her off her feet."

The comment about something from his personal life made her hungry to hear more. "What happened to her husband?"

A bleak look entered his eyes. "Chaz was flying his light plane when he ran into bad weather over the Alps and crashed."

"Oh how awful," Darrell whispered, strangely moved by everything he said or did.

"It was one of the worst moments of my life," he confessed.

She could hear the pain in his voice. "How old are his children?"

"Nine and ten."

"Such vulnerable ages. My heart goes out to them and their mother."

In the midst of the silence they heard Phillip say, "What are their names?"

They both turned in his direction.

Alex had been right to leave him be. His curiosity over his father had won out. No telling how long he'd been listening on the other side of the doorway. Darrell didn't dare breathe while her son's whole attention was focused on his fascinating father.

Alex glanced at him while he finished rinsing off the plates. "Jules and Vito."

"One of the guys in my French class is named Jules. We all had to pick a name."

Alex folded the dish towel. "What did you choose?"

"Philippe."

"That's your grandfather's name."

"I thought that was *your* name."

"It's one of them. But my mother and closest friends call me Alex so there's no confusion."

Phillip took another step closer. "Is he still alive?"

"No. He died six years ago. But your grandmother is very much alive. Her name is Katerina."

"If you could never find my mother, how do you know about me?"

"Because I went searching for your father," Darrell declared.

Phillip looked at her in disbelief. "But I thought you didn't know anything about him."

"I didn't. But he gave your mom a very unique ring. I'd forgotten about it until a few weeks ago."

That was a lie of course. The ring had haunted her for years, but it would still be in her old coat pocket if Phillip had let go of his pain.

"I decided to have it traced…and found your father."

"When?" Phillip demanded.

"Yesterday."

His astounded gaze switched back to his father. "You live in Chicago? I thought you were from New York."

Darrell shook her head. "No, sweetheart. I never went to Chicago or New York."

"I don't get it."

"Maybe this will help." Alex pulled the ring from his pocket and handed it to Phillip who took it and began examining it with interest.

"This looks like a knight's shield."

"That's exactly what it is," Alex asserted. "My cousin, Chaz, gave it to me when I turned sixteen. He had it engraved. It says, 'More than a cousin.' The shield represents the coat of arms of our family."

Finally Phillip raised his head. "Where do you live?"

"Switzerland."

Surprise and wonder broke out on Phillip's face. "That's where they speak four different languages. I learned about that in my French class. Which one do you speak?"

"All of them," Alex answered.

"Even that funny one called Romanish or something?"

Alex smiled broadly, causing Darrell's heart to flip over. "Especially that one."

"How come?"

"Because my home is in Bris, the heart of the Romanche-speaking Canton. It might interest you to know there are five forms of Romanche, a language dating back to Roman times."

"Do you speak those, too?"

"Yes."

It was too much for anyone to absorb, especially a young American teen who'd just been united with the father he'd always wanted to meet.

"When I had to leave Colorado, I gave that ring to your mother to remember me by. It's a family heirloom. Now it's yours, Phillip. No one else in the world is entitled to wear it unless they're a Valleder."

"A Valleder?"

"Yes. If your mother and I had married, your legal name would be Phillip Collier Valleder. If you've got some tape, I'll fix it so you can wear it now."

"There's some in the drawer." Phillip opened it and handed the dispenser to Alex. In a minute the ring slid on his finger and stayed put.

Her son's eyes squinted up at him. Darrell could hear his mind working. "What's your legal name?"

"Alexandre Rainier Juliani Phillip Vittorio Valleder."

"Whoa."

A deep laugh escaped Alex's throat. It was so contagious Phillip smiled. Darrell hadn't seen one like it in years...

But when the laughter died down, Phillip grew sober again. "Do you have a wife and kids?"

Alex's eyes were hooded as he said, "You're my only child."

"But at the end of this month he's getting married to a woman named Isabella," Darrell informed her son to make certain he understood the situation in no uncertain terms.

After reflection Phillip said quietly, "Did you love my mom?"

CHAPTER THREE

THE question had been thrown out like a live wire.

Alex put his hands on Phillip's shoulders. "We only knew each other for a few days. Not long enough to find out our deepest feelings. But we were obviously attracted enough to spend all our free time together. I wish I'd known about you."

Darrell felt his thick-toned voice resonate to her bones.

"Whether you believe me or not, I'm thrilled to discover I have a son. This is the most exciting moment of my life. I couldn't get here fast enough. I love you, Philippe." The admission came out as naturally as the French version of Phillip's name.

After a throbbing silence Phillip whispered, "I'm sorry for what I said to you earlier. I...love you, too."

In the next breath both of them were hugging. They held on to each other for a long time.

The moment was so profoundly tender, Darrell pressed a hand against the strange pain in her chest.

"What would you like to do about our situation?" Alex asked once he'd finally let his son go.

Phillip stared up at him with a new light shining from his eyes. "Will you come and visit me sometimes?"

"Of course."

"Can I come and visit you sometimes?"

"Whenever you want. It's up to your mother."

Phillip flicked her a glance she couldn't decipher. Then he looked at Alex again. "How long are you going to stay in Denver?"

"I have to fly back to Switzerland tonight." While Darrell's heart plummeted for Phillip's sake, Alex unexpectedly said, "How would you like to come with me and see where I live? That invitation includes your mother. You're welcome to stay with me for as long as you want."

"Mom—"

Phillip was ready to burst with joy.

Darrell knew what he was asking, but everything was happening way too fast.

"I'm afraid you can't go right now, sweetheart. For one thing you don't have a passport."

Alex eyed her with a direct stare. "That's no problem. Trust me."

Of course it wasn't a problem. He was the king. He could let anyone in his kingdom he wanted. It appeared he wanted his son.

"What's the other thing?" Alex challenged her.

He knew exactly why she was holding back! The news about Phillip would be like a hundred megaton bomb exploding in his country.

How could he just get off his private jet with a son in tow no one had ever seen or heard of? Surely he would want to prepare his family first. His fiancée most of all…

Darrell tried to put herself in the other woman's place. The shock of learning the king she was going to marry came complete with a twelve-year-old son would destroy her dreams of starting out marriage in the hope of raising a family of her own.

"Phillip? Remember that Danice asked us to spend the Fourth with her?"

"But I told you I don't want to go."

Alex flicked her a penetrating glance. "You have other plans made?"

She averted her eyes. "Not yet. That call in the kitchen was Danice phoning to finalize everything." She could feel both of them looking at her, yet neither said a word. Already father and son were in lockstep.

The onus was on Darrell. If she said no to Phillip, he wouldn't understand. Not when she'd gone all the way to Switzerland to find his father.

Now that she'd achieved her goal, a whole new range of problems loomed over the horizon. She was starting to get scared and Alex knew it.

"Tell you what, Phillip. I'll go out to the limo so you and your mother can talk in private." He was reading her mind. "Come outside when you're ready and let me know what you've decided."

"Thank you, Alex," she murmured.

"But, Mom—"

In a few swift strides his father left the house. Phillip turned to her ready to do battle.

"Before you say anything to me, young man, I want to ask you a question." He blinked. "What else did your French teacher tell you about the Romanche-speaking canton?"

He blinked again and shrugged his shoulders. "I don't remember."

"It's ruled by a king."

"That's cool."

"Cool doesn't begin to cover it. Your father has a very important job which is different from the jobs of any of your friends' dads."

"What is it?"

"Did your teacher happen to mention the name of that particular canton?"

"No."

She drew in a deep breath. "It's the Valleder Canton."

He cocked his head. "That's Dad's last name."

"That's right. Your dad…is the king of Valleder."

Phillip let out a bark of laughter. "No, he's not."

That had been Darrell's reaction when she'd first read the information on the Internet.

"Your father's waiting for us. We better hurry and get packed."

She started up the stairs. He was close on her heels.

"Mom—come on. You're joking, right?"

She kept on going.

"Mom?"

She pulled his suitcase out of the hall closet before hurrying into his room and opening drawers.

"Some dads drive buses, others are engineers, lots of them run businesses…and a select few on the planet rule over their own country. I thought I'd let you know that before you run outside and tell him we're going with him.

"Once we reach the airport, I don't want you to be surprised when you hear his staff and security people call him 'Your Majesty.'"

Five minutes after Alex climbed in the limousine, Phillip came flying down the walkway toward him. The resemblance between them shouted his paternity. Alex suffered pain to realize he'd already lost twelve years with him. Only now could he appreciate Chaz's joy when Vito was born.

"I can't describe the feeling, Alex. You'll have to have a child of your own to understand what it's like!"

At last Alex knew exactly what it was like. He had his own

wonderful child. Incredible. Phillip was his son! Realizing he was a father filled his world with possibilities he'd never considered before.

Phillip opened the door. "We're coming with you! Mom said to give us about twenty more minutes."

The excitement those words engendered caused Alex to shove every other concern to the back of his mind. "Take all the time you need."

Phillip scrutinized him for a moment. "Mom told me something else, but I didn't believe her."

His son expressed himself exactly like young Jules. That was because they both had Valleder blood flowing through their veins.

"I didn't believe it, either, when my father who was dying said, 'Alex? Promise me you'll look after your mother and be a good king.'"

There was another full minute of silence before a hint of devilry entered Phillip's eyes. "Did it freak you out to be a king at first?"

Just then Phillip sounded so much like Chaz, Alex was dumbfounded. When they'd buried Chaz, Alex never expected to see traces of his cousin come to life in Alex's own son.

"Don't tell this to anybody, but it still freaks me out."

"You have to worry about terrorism and stuff, huh."

For a twelve-year-old, Phillip understood too much.

"It's part of my job, but certainly not all."

Phillip studied him. "Mom told me you're getting married to a princess." After a slight hesitation, "I wish my real mom hadn't died."

With that comment Alex was beginning to understand the burning issue Darrell had been forced to deal with over the years where Phillip was concerned. Having a son who had been deprived of his birth parents and suffered over it couldn't have been easy for Darrell who'd devoted her life to raising him.

His brows knit together. "I'm sorry, too, but look at it this way. You've been lucky enough to have *two* real moms, Phillip. Your second mother loves you so much, she came looking for me and wouldn't stop until she found me." In fact she'd taken a dangerous risk. The analogy of the mother and the burning building was no joke.

"Think how happy her efforts have made you and me. She didn't have to do anything at all. In fact another kind of mother might not have spent her time and hard-earned money to make your wish come true."

Hoping Phillip would think long and hard on that he added, "Why don't you go inside and see if she needs any help. After her long flights to Switzerland and back, she must be exhausted."

She'd put her son's welfare before anything else. What an amazing woman she was…

Phillip appeared more subdued before he nodded and hurried back to the condo.

The moment he disappeared inside, Alex pulled out his cell phone to alert his pilot, then tell his security staff he was ready to leave with Ms. Collier and her son.

Once that was taken care of, he phoned Carl. If there'd been anything urgent from his private secretary's end, Alex would have heard from him by now.

"I'll be home in the morning, Carl. Do me a favor and tell the staff to get the Saxony apartment ready by the time I arrive back in Bris."

"I'll see to it at once, Your Majesty. I understand Princess Isabella has a preference for daffodils. Shall I arrange for some?"

Alex's hand gripped his cell phone tighter. "You've misunderstood me, Carl. I'll be bringing my twelve-year-old son and his mother with me. Fill the drawing room with white roses, and make certain there are plenty of snack foods and fruit drinks on hand for Phillip."

"Phillip?" Carl whispered in an unsteady voice.

Alex couldn't help but smile. He'd always wondered if the secretary who'd worked for Alex's father and was loyal to him could be shaken by anything.

Now he knew he'd given the sixty-year-old man a minor coronary. This was only the beginning, but no force could stop him now. Phillip needed his father. Alex found he didn't like the idea of any other man taking over that role no matter the consequences of his actions.

"Until I tell my mother, I know I can count on your discretion, Carl."

"Of course, Your Majesty."

After the click, Alex made his last phone call for the night.

"Leo? Sorry to waken you, but I thought you'd like to know the crisis has been averted."

"So she doesn't pose a threat?"

"No," he lied.

"Thank God."

"As it turns out, she's the mother of my son, but thirteen years ago she was a girl who has changed a great deal since then."

"Sorry, Alex. We must have a bad connection and I heard you wrong. Say that again."

The connection was perfect.

"Darrell Collier has been raising my son for the last twelve years. I'm afraid I parted with that ring one starry night in the Colorado mountains where she was working for the summer. But as I told you, the memory is vague due to too much alcohol on both our parts.

"When Uncle Vittorio had a bad accident while I was on vacation with Chaz, we had to fly home. Since I traveled incognito, Ms. Collier didn't know who I was or where to reach me. So we never saw each other again. For Phillip's sake she's been trying to find me."

He heard the other man make a strange sound in his throat. "You call this a crisis averted?" Leo blurted in genuine alarm. "After hearing news of this magnitude, how in the hell are you even functioning?"

"I admit I was in shock until Phillip came running in Darrell's house. He's a living miracle, Leo. I'm bringing him and his mother home with me tonight."

"What?"

"I'm his father. He's never given up hope of being united with me."

"Obviously Ms. Collier never got over you, either, or she'd be married by now."

Alex let the remark go. For the moment it was too complicated to explain about Melissa, let alone Darrell's sacrifice. For several reasons no one could know the truth yet. Darrell was Phillip's legal mother. For the time being that was as much as Alex wanted anyone to know.

First and foremost, he needed Darrell with them in order to establish a bond with his son.

"It's only natural he wants to see where I live and spend time with me. We need to get acquainted, but I can't do that in Denver while I have so many commitments back in Bris right now."

"Alex—you're not thinking like a king whose marriage is three weeks away. You haven't thought through the myriad ramifications."

That was all Alex *had* been doing. But no matter what he had to face, it took a back seat to the joy he'd felt when Phillip let go of his pain and hugged him. An inexplicable sense of their belonging together had assailed him. At that moment his gratitude to Darrell knew no limits.

"Who else knows about this besides me?"

"Carl. But he's the soul of discretion."

"How much does Phillip look like you?"

"The second you meet him, you'll know he's mine."

By the silence, Alex could tell Leo was still trying to absorb the earthshaking news. Finally he said, "I'll make certain bodyguards are assigned to them."

"Thanks, Leo."

"Alex—I'm not speaking as your security advisor now, but as your friend. Take my advice and don't bring them to Bris until after your wedding. Then it can be handled privately. Give this more time or the press will tear you to pieces."

Not just the press, Alex muttered inwardly. His uncle Vittorio, the second most powerful man in the kingdom, would be outraged and poison the cabinet against Alex, forcing him to step down. Fortunately he was still in Greece on a cruise with Alex's Aunt Renate.

As for Alex's mother, she would go into shock. But he had faith she would recover. He had a plan how he would handle Isabella's parents. Which brought him around to thoughts of Isabella and her reaction. This news would crush her in ways he didn't want to entertain. There was no way around the fact that Alex was about to do an unthinkable thing to her...

But the truly unthinkable thing would be to turn his back on his son. Already Phillip had a stranglehold on his heart that took precedence over every other consideration.

He lowered his head. "If I don't follow through, Phillip will take it as a rejection, Leo. I can't risk it. He's too emotionally vulnerable."

After twelve years Alex had to act immediately or he could never hope to have a close relationship with his newfound son.

"Isabella's going to find out!"

"I intend to tell her the truth before she hears it from another source."

"That's a terrifying thought, Alex."

Leo was wrong. The only terrifying thought was that Phillip had been alive all these years and Alex hadn't known about it. He closed his eyes for a moment, thankful that Darrell's love for Phillip had driven her to unite him and Alex.

"I want him with me forever. I love him, Leo."

"Understood," his friend whispered at last. "But you *are* the king. My first instinct is to want to protect you. Hell, Alex, I'm sorry to have come at you like this. I have no right."

"No man had a better friend. That gives you the right. If this had happened to you, I'd be voicing the same concerns."

"What in the name of heaven are you going to do?"

From the limo window Alex could see the lights go out in the upstairs portion of the condo. His security people had started to close in.

"The only thing I can do. Take it a step at a time." Alex had never been a father before. He needed time for the wonder of it to sink in. There were plans to make. "We'll talk when I land."

After ringing off, Alex levered himself from the back of the limo in order to help Darrell, who'd just locked her front door. He was glad to see that Phillip was carrying both their bags. Two security men offered to assist him but Phillip held on to them all the way to the limo.

Alex's first little parental talk with his son had produced results. His heart swelled with fatherly pride. Too many emotions were welling inside of him from all directions.

As Darrell walked toward Alex, the glow from the street lamps highlighted the silvery-gold sheen of her hair.

Unable to keep from studying the contours of her lovely face and figure, he felt the same quickening in his blood as before when she'd first walked up the steps of the jet. To his chagrin it was much stronger now.

The fact that he'd never had this kind of reaction to Isabella caused him to groan because he knew he was in trouble. Worse, there wasn't a damn thing he wanted to do about it. What in heaven's name was happening to him?

Darrell discovered there were two bedrooms aboard the plane. For the flight to Switzerland Alex had installed them in the one normally reserved for his mother. When Phillip joked about the queen-size bed being named after his grandmother, laughter pealed out of Alex.

Though he indulged his son and seemed to find him a never ending source of entertainment, Darrell was concerned Phillip's sometimes cheeky nature was too over the top.

He hadn't inherited that behavioral trait from Melissa, so Darrell had assumed he must be more like his father. But Alex wasn't anything like Phillip in that regard, which made Darrell wonder where exactly the imp in Phillip had come from.

After he'd changed into sweats and climbed under the covers he looked up at Darrell. "Dad's awesome."

The hero-worship in her son's eyes was clear for anyone to see. For the last hour Phillip had fired one outrageous question after another at his father until they were all worn out from laughing.

"I agree."

"My friends are going to freak when they find out he's the king of Valleder."

"You're right about that. Just remember that for now it's our secret, and we're simply your father's guests. The woman he's going to marry doesn't know about you yet. After he's told her, then you can claim him."

"You don't think she's going to like me, huh."

Darrell struggled for the right words. "I doubt your father would choose a woman who wouldn't like you, but she's going to need time to get used to the idea that she has to share him with you." All of three little weeks in fact.

"Why? Steve's stepmom likes *him*."

"I'm sure in time Isabella will come to love you, sweetheart. But she's a princess who's been planning to marry your father for a long time. She doesn't know he has a son. It's going to be a shock to her."

The whole thing was a shock to Darrell who couldn't get Alex's image out of her mind. What was wrong with her to be thinking intimate thoughts about a betrothed king who'd once slept with her sister? None of it made sense!

Phillip frowned. "Do you think Dad wishes you'd never found him?"

"No," she said without hesitation. "Otherwise you wouldn't be on his royal jet right now."

He sighed. "Dad said he's glad I'm learning French. He keeps calling me Phillip."

"Of course. One of these years he'll have you speaking Italian and German and Romanche, too."

"He's super intelligent. No matter what you ask him, he knows all about it."

She nodded. "From the day he was born, he was tutored by experts to be king one day. He has to be on top of everything."

Being a father to a child he hadn't known about would have thrown any other man, let alone a king. Yet he'd let nothing stand in the way. Darrell had a foreboding there was going to be a huge price Alex would have to pay. It terrified her.

"Someday I'm going to be as smart as he is."

"You're his son, so I wouldn't be surprised. But you'll have to start taking your homework more seriously."

"I know."

She turned out the light. "I'm going to say good-night to him, then I'll be back."

"Okay."

Her fear for the whole situation caused her to leave the cabin for the den where the three of them had been talking earlier. Alex was just coming out.

They would have collided but for his quick reflexes that sent his hands to her shoulders to steady her.

She let out a small cry of surprise.

"That was close," he murmured without relinquishing his hold on her.

"Yes." She exhaled the word, afraid to look at him. Even though the jet was full of his staff, in the dimly lit passageway it felt like the two of them were far removed from the rest of his entourage.

His male warmth enhanced the tang of the soap he used, overwhelming her with telltale sensations and yearnings.

A long time ago Melissa had experienced these same feelings. With the help of alcohol she'd acted on them and he'd been willing. To Darrell's shame, she couldn't seem to control her attraction to the man who'd given Melissa a son.

If he'd been a normal man who'd married her sister, Alex would be her brother-in-law. Instead he was engaged to be married to another royal. Darrell needed to keep that fact foremost in her mind. He was off-limits to her and always would be.

Guilt drove her to back away from him, forcing his hands to let go of her.

"I know it's late," she said in a breathless voice, "but now that Phillip's in bed, there's something we have to talk about."

"If you're referring to our son, he seemed fine to me earlier."

"I agree. I'm afraid I'm the one who's nervous. My relationship with Phillip is changing. When I think of the life we've had in Denver all these years. Now everything's different."

Her head fell back as she looked up at him through eyes that had turned a deeper shade of violet. "I keep wondering what I've gotten us into. I—I'm scared."

His lips tightened, giving him a forbidding aura that made her tremble.

"What are you really saying, Darrell? You want me to instruct my pilot to turn the jet around?"

"No—Yes—" she cried, covering her face with her hands, "This is going to ruin your life—" The words came out muffled.

To her surprise he removed her hands. Still holding them clasped in his he said, "Look at me."

She was afraid to, but his compelling demand had her lifting her chin. His gaze probed hers.

"The fact of Phillip's existence trumps all royal oaths and pledges. There's no question this is going to change things. But I'll make you this promise. I'll do everything in my power to shield Phillip from any unnecessary hurt."

Darrell could hardly swallow. Once again she eased herself away from his touch.

"Melissa begged me to look for you because she believed in you. Now that I've found you, I believe in you. I know you'll do everything in your power to make Phillip feel secure in your love. But I'm not naïve.

"Though I may not have been born to royalty, I've read enough history over the years to know the normal challenges of living take on a life of their own within a royal household.

"I have to admit I'm afraid for all of us. For you! Your wedding day should be one of happiness and joy. If the monarchy suffers, then I'm going to feel responsible. So I'm begging you to rethink what you're doing. It's still not too late to go back to Denver and give this a little more time."

He stared at her through shuttered eyes. "It was too late the moment I saw the pictures of the ring. I'm the one who set things in motion thirteen years ago. Therefore that absolves you of all responsibility. As I told you earlier, I can never repay you for restoring my son to me. Perhaps he'll be the only son I ever have, the only child...

"Since no man can know what the future holds, we'll think only the best thoughts."

The best thoughts? her heart cried hysterically.

"Just so you know what to expect ahead of time, a helicopter will be waiting at the airport in Zurich to fly you to the castle. You'll be taken to one of the apartments on the second floor, which has been prepared for you and Phillip.

"Anything you need, whether it's food or fresh towels, all you have to do is pick up the phone and press line two. Rudy will see to your requests and arrange a morning city tour for you. It will give Phillip a feel for the place.

"To reach me, press line one and my private secretary Carl will get word to me. I plan to join you at the pool by midafternoon for a swim and an early dinner."

"Where will you be until then so I can tell Phillip?"

She watched his broad chest rise and fall. "San Ravino."

"Is that where the princess lives?"

"Yes. By noon tomorrow she'll have heard the truth from me in person."

"Oh, Alex—" she cried softly, forgetting she wasn't going to look at him. "Isn't there anything I can say to get you to reconsider acting too hastily?"

"No."

Darrell moaned because a chiseled mask slipped over his striking features. She could feel it lock into place like the suits of battle armor on display in his castle's ancient war room.

"The matter's settled, Ms. Collier."

In an instant he'd put an impenetrable barrier between them, one that froze her out with devastating force.

For a few minutes she'd forgotten he was a king and had pled with the man. But she wouldn't be making that mistake again. "Good night, Your Majesty."

Darrell hurried down the corridor to the bedroom. Almost crazy from lack of sleep and the incredible circumstances of their lives, she got ready for bed in the dark, then slid under the covers, taking care not to disturb Phillip. Before long oblivion took over.

Toward morning her troubled dreams had changed into a nightmare. At one point she came awake in a cold sweat with the very real premonition that the fairy tale Melissa had envisioned would not end in the traditional manner.

In Darrell's dream she was hidden in the crowd of spectators lining the streets on Alex's wedding day. The disillusioned citizens of his kingdom were booing the broken king and his twelve-year-old American offshoot sitting in the carriage between him and his grieving queen.

Quickly, before Phillip woke up and asked her why her face was wet, she rushed into the bathroom to shower. When she emerged a few minutes later, he was awake. The room steward had already delivered their breakfast trays, but Phillip's was still untouched.

"How come you're not eating?" she asked as she pulled a hydrangea blue two-piece suit from her luggage.

"I'm not hungry."

That had to be a first for him.

"In that case, you'd better shower."

"Okay." He rolled out of bed. "I can't wait to see Dad."

"I'm sure he feels the same way, but he's a busy man, so you're going to have to be patient."

"I know."

No. Phillip didn't know. He didn't have a clue, and patience was not his strong suit.

Alex had been inspired to suggest a tour of the city. The key to handling Phillip's nervous energy was to keep him busy, something his father seemed to understand instinctively.

For herself Darrell was glad they would be kept so occupied she wouldn't have a lot of time to imagine what was happening in San Ravino.

She shuddered to think of the princess who was probably eating breakfast right now with no idea that in a few hours her whole world was going to be shattered.

CHAPTER FOUR

"WHOA, Mom!" Phillip's hungry eyes had just taken in the setting of the medieval castle at Bris, bordered in back by Lake Bris. Darrell's heart echoed his words as the helicopter set them down on a helipad amidst the private, velvety green grounds east of the massive stone structure.

Accompanied by bodyguards who'd taken pains to explain everything they were seeing during their flight from Zurich, it truly was like being in a fantastic dream. From this height she could see other parts hidden from the public to the west that included a palace, a stable, tennis courts and a swimming pool.

On Darrell's first visit to the castle the other day, she'd had to stand in line with other tourists at the front entrance, and saw but a small portion of the magnificent royal estate. Only from the air could you appreciate its vast size and splendor originating from the Middle Ages when the earliest Valleder kings built the city's stronghold to keep the enemy at bay.

From the ticket window she'd followed the guide straight down to the vaulted, lonely dungeons every tourist came to see. But the tour had passed in a blur because her mind had been focused on meeting Phillip's father. Such wasn't the case with her son this morning. All Darrell had to do was look at his face to realize he couldn't wait to go exploring in those dark, dank places. This was his legacy after all.

For her the real wonder of the castle lay in the rooms upstairs where the public was never allowed to go. Rudy, the man named who'd been on Alex's staff for years and spoke excellent English, met them at the base of the grand staircase. He took over and gave them a cursory tour on the way to their room.

Both she and Phillip marveled at the grand knights' halls, the secret twisting passages between lavish bedchambers, the Gothic windows with glorious views, a large, frescoed chapel. There was so much to see, it would take weeks!

"The Grand Kitchen," Rudy explained, "still has its original wooden ceiling and four massive oak pillars which were installed in 1270." He showed them the Plessur Bedchamber containing the original bird and ribbon decorations dating from the 1580s. When he escorted them to the expansive Hall of Arms covered with escutcheons of the Valleder bailiffs, Phillip went into ecstasy and didn't want to leave. But Rudy reminded him, "There's much more to see."

He was right. The King's Chamber with its original thirteenth-century wall paintings showed rustic scenes of animals in a meadow with St. George slaying a beast on the chimneypiece. Not far from that room they entered the magnificent Great Hall of the Prince of Bris with its original octagonal table and tapestries.

Finally Rudy escorted them to the Saxony apartment where they would be staying. It was two bedrooms really, both with enormous canopied beds and fireplaces, and joined by a set of carved doors. "This is awesome!" Phillip exclaimed. Rudy laughed, obviously finding her son amusing. But Darrell was so overcome by the room's beauty, she stood in place, speechless.

There were slender black marble pillars and shimmering checkered wall decorations. Her neck hurt from viewing the coffered ceilings, which dated from the fourteenth century. She was charmed by the two recessed windows with window seats overlooking the lake. Above the arches of each window was a fabulous cloverleaf design. The same set of windows graced the smaller, adjoining room. Exquisite.

"Hey, Mom— Come here! Your room has a balcony!"

Rudy had opened a pair of doors that went from the inlaid-wood floor to the vaulted ceiling. The inserts told a Biblical story in gorgeous stained glass. Beyond them lay the shimmering waters of Lake Bris.

The sculptured stone balcony could have been made for Romeo and Juliet. It hung out over the water, taking her breath. So did the view of the mountains rising from the other side of the lake.

"His Majesty asked me to take you on a tour of the city. I'll come by for you in twenty minutes. In the meantime, make yourselves at home. Your bags have been brought up."

Once Rudy had gone, Phillip let out a whoop of excitement and began exploring his room. He soon discovered a mini-fridge had been installed. It was filled with drinks and treats. "Dad's the best! I wish he hadn't had to leave."

"You know why he did."

"Yeah… I can't wait to see him!"

Darrell felt the same way. Alex's presence had an electric effect on her, but she kept those thoughts to herself.

Later in the day she lay in the sun on one of the pool loungers. She'd put on a pair of denim shorts and a white halter top. When a shadow fell across her, she thought Phillip had come back outside after going to their apartment for a snack. Following the sightseeing visit of Bris he'd grown tired of waiting for his father, and had rediscovered his appetite.

But when she opened her eyes, she had to look up a long way before she encountered a pair of eyes that were intensely alive and had taken on the green of the immaculate lawn. They'd been studying the lines and curves of her body without her realizing it. A tiny gasp escaped her throat.

The excitement of seeing Alex made her pulse race until she remembered his meeting with Isabella, which had to be one of the worst moments of their lives. Yet Darrell couldn't tell by his demeanor how he'd been affected. He was like the proverbial rock you could cling to no matter the fury of the storm.

She noted inconsequentially he was wearing a silky Ceylon-blue shirt with beige trousers. In danger of staring at the hard male lines of his unforgettable face, she got up from the lounger dragging the towel in front of her. Though her outfit was perfectly modest, the way his gaze traveled over her body and slender legs caused her to feel exposed.

Before she could gather her wits he said, "Forgive me for arriving late, but it couldn't be helped. Where's our son?"

Anyone hearing him would assume she and Alex were man and wife. Thank goodness no one was around except his security people who'd positioned themselves at a discreet distance.

"He got hungry and went back to the apartment."

"How do you like your accommodations?"

The question threw her because he was avoiding the subject of Isabella. It made Darrell want to cry out in exasperation. But as she'd learned to her chagrin last night, he couldn't be moved by begging or pleading.

"Surely you already know the answer to that. I've never been in a more beautiful set of rooms in my life. The balcony overlooking the lake makes me feel like I'm living in a medieval tapestry. Undoubtedly the chatelaine of the castle, one of your female progenitors, stood in that very spot watching for her knight to return from battle.

"Before I came outside I must have spent at least an hour examining the stories in the stained glass."

His eyes gleamed with satisfaction. "What does Phillip think of things so far?"

"He just keeps walking around examining everything and saying 'whoa' every few seconds. Unfortunately he's already told me how cool it would be to attach a rope from the balcony and lower himself into the blue depths, which must be hundreds of feet below."

A mysterious light entered Alex's eyes. "I know someone who once did that very thing and got into a lot of trouble for it. Great minds think alike."

Forgetting that he could be implacable, she cried, "Alex— please don't keep me in suspense any longer. I have to know what happened today!"

He held her imploring gaze. "The princess came back to Bris with me."

Darrell could scarcely credit what he'd just told her. "She's here? At the castle?"

"Yes. She wants to meet Phillip. I think it would be best if she met him before being introduced to you."

Her hands crushed the toweling. Darrell couldn't be jealous of the woman he was about to marry. She just couldn't be! "Of course."

She knew it was for the best, but it hurt because she could already feel Phillip slipping away from her. It surprised her how possessive of him she was. But then her maternal instincts had never been tested to this degree before.

He was Alex's son, too. She'd better get used to sharing him. Yet the thought of the two of them enjoying each other's company in the presence of Isabella left Darrell feeling oddly bereft.

"I've arranged for the three of us to dine informally within the hour. I'll walk you back to the apartment to get him."

If Darrell were prone to fainting spells, she'd be sprawled across the pool tiles by now.

For Isabella to be willing to meet Phillip meant she was so madly in love with Alex, she'd put up with anything to become his wife, even if she was dying inside. Under the circumstances of their approaching wedding, that was the best news possible for Alex.

"She must be a wonderful person."

He nodded. "She's remarkable."

Of course he would never tell Darrell about the pain and the tears that had gone on behind closed doors before his fiancée had made the decision to face this crisis head-on. Already Isabella was showing a queenly composure Alex could only marvel at.

"I hope Phillip makes a good impression." Her voice trembled. "Naturally you and I both love him, but you know how unpredictable he can be at times."

"It's one of his most endearing qualities," Alex stated matter-of-factly. "Isabella will find him intriguing."

Spoken like a proud father who accepted his son without qualification.

It thrilled Darrell that Alex loved him so much. However it would take time for Isabella to develop a relationship with him. The thought of Phillip having a stepmother brought a sharp pain to her heart, one she needed to squelch in a hurry.

By tacit agreement they started walking toward the entrance leading to the Saxony apartment. As the castle loomed before her, the old adage about a man's home being his castle brought a faint smile to one corner of her mouth.

"What are you thinking about?" He noticed everything. When Darrell told him, he chuckled.

"I'm still having trouble believing all this is real," she confessed with a sigh. "To think that several days ago I was in line with other tourists outside the castle, trying to imagine your world. Little did I know what lay in store once you recognized the ring," her voice throbbed.

"Your arrival shook my world, too, Darrell. I'll never be the same again. You do realize you've raised a surprisingly unspoiled child."

"I don't know about that, but he *is* an original thinker. When he realizes Isabella is younger than his friends' mothers, he'll like that a lot." She needed to keep her thoughts centered on the princess. "Does she have siblings?"

"Yes. A brother two years her senior."

"Then she's been broken in"

A half smile creased the corner of his male mouth. "Most definitely."

"Knowing that will please Phillip. He'll want to meet him. You know. Get the inside scoop on what it's like to live with a princess."

The low laughter she loved rolled out of Alex. "I can see you've never had a dull moment with him."

She sent him an unguarded smile. "Dull is the one adjective that will never apply to Phillip."

He opened the door for her. "I envy you all those years with him."

By the depth of his tone, she knew he meant it. "If you want to know a secret, I don't think he'll ever forgive me for not looking for you sooner."

His eyes darkened with emotion. "Thank God you found a way to get my attention. You were incredibly courageous and resourceful. If my father were alive, he would tell you you're one of those rare female warriors upon whom future generations depend to raise up worthy sons."

Darrell half scoffed. She wondered if any woman had ever received such an unusual compliment.

Deep in thought she moved past him, but her shoulder accidentally brushed against his chest. Little sparks of fire crackled through her nervous system. She hurried up the stairs ahead of him so he wouldn't see how shallow her breathing had become.

Even though it had only been for one night, Alex had been her sister's lover. Her awareness of that fact intensified her guilt in ways she didn't want to explore right now.

It was a good thing she wouldn't be going to dinner with the three of them. The more she was around Alex, the harder it would be to keep her attraction to him a secret, especially from Isabella, who was about to become his wife.

A woman in love sensed when another woman was interested in her man.

Of course the princess had no worry in that regard. Alex was pledged to her. Their future marriage had been decreed and settled years earlier. Darrell was an idiot to go on entertaining forbidden thoughts about him.

"Phillip?" she called out after entering the apartment. "Your father's back!"

When he didn't answer, she hurried through the door to the adjoining room where he planned to sleep. "He's not here!" She turned to Alex. "I don't know where he'd be."

Something close to a grin broke out on his rugged features. "Considering it's our son, we both know the possibilities are endless. But you don't need to worry. He's been assigned a bodyguard. I'll call him."

While he pulled out his cell phone, Darrell went over to the armoire where one of the maids had hung Phillip's clothes. She picked out the navy blazer and khaki's he wore to church. Even if Alex said the dinner would be informal, she wanted Phillip to be on his best behavior in front of Isabella.

After reaching for his white shirt and striped tie, she took everything over to the bed.

Alex spoke in Romanche, preventing her from understanding him. She had to wait until he'd hung up.

"Where did he go?"

"After touring the dungeon, he went to Carl's office. They're having an off-the-record chat about what it's like to work for me."

"Oh, no— Does Carl know Phill—"

"Yes," Alex broke in, reading her mind with ease.

"Everyone must know by now. You two look too much alike to deceive anyone."

One of his expressive brows quirked. "The family resemblance is strong. As you said earlier, the water has spilled over the dam. There's no putting it back."

She moaned. "You put on a brave front, but I know deep down you have to be apprehensive about everyone's reaction."

"You're wrong, Darrell. My biggest concern is that when the novelty wears off, Phillip won't like it here, and he'll want to go home."

She couldn't believe he'd just said that.

"Alex—he has already bonded with you. It's uncanny how well you get along and understand him."

"It's because I see certain traits of my cousin Chaz in him. He'll never be a conformist."

"You're right, but that won't prevent him from wanting to spend as much time with you as possible."

Lines marred his features. "You just hit on the problem."

"I—I don't understand," her voice caught.

"I may be his father, but I'm also the king. The two don't necessarily mesh."

Her anxious gaze swerved to his. "Weren't you and your father close?"

"If you mean did we love and respect each other, then yes. But it was never the kind of relationship you're envisioning.

Father was the king. He belonged to every man. I was a typical selfish child who wanted him to myself.

"Phillip's been deprived of his father all these years. Now that we've found each other I'm afraid he's going to feel cheated in a brand-new way. I would understand if he didn't want to hang around waiting to spend time with me. That's what is haunting me."

Put like that Darrell was haunted too. Not just for Phillip who *had* been hanging around all day waiting, but for Alex.

He'd just revealed something of his inner struggle as a child. He'd said it with a hunger that bespoke needs as strong in their own right as his son's. She would never have guessed...

"But he knows you came to get him the second you found out you had a son. You didn't let your kingly duties stand in the way. You're one man in a million to have claimed him in front of everyone. He feels loved."

"I pray to God that's true," he murmured.

"It is, and it's all he ever wanted. Just try to get rid of him now and see what happens," she teased to cover her emotions.

His expression grew solemn. "Where did you come from, Darrell Collier?"

The pounding of her heart almost suffocated her. "That's the question I've been asking about you since we met aboard your jet. The chance of your world and Melissa's colliding is so remote as to be almost impossible, yet it happened."

If she kept the vision of him and her sister wrapped up in his sleeping bag, she might just make it through this painful experience without revealing her inner turmoil.

His chest rose and fell visibly. "I have to be honest and tell you the memory of that night is so vague that without the photos proving the existence of the ring, I wouldn't have recalled it."

"So what you told Phillip wasn't completely true."

He rubbed his bottom lip with his thumb. "If you mean that I spent as much time as possible with your sister, then no. Nor did I try to get in touch with her again. There was only the one night, but Phillip didn't need to know that."

Darrell hugged that piece of information to her heart. "I agree."

"Chaz and a girl who worked at the ranch fixed me up with your sister. We went to a local bar and began drinking. One thing led to another.

"I'm not proud of my behavior, Darrell. Obviously I'd decided to do a little rebelling against my gilded cage. But the next day as I nursed a hangover all the way back to Switzerland, I vowed never to put myself or another woman in that position again. You have every right to hate me for what I did."

"Of course I don't hate you. That rebellion produced a wonderful boy. He's my life!" her voice shook.

In fact knowing Melissa was simply a girl who happened to be there at the right time and place verified Darrell's opinion that all the feeling had been on her sister's part. Otherwise Alex would have come back to Colorado to take up where he'd left off.

The knowledge that Melissa wasn't the great love of his life gave Darrell a lot to think about. To be betrothed to a princess who was only thirteen at the time meant Isabella hadn't started out as his great love, either. But that obviously changed when she grew into the woman he adored.

Alex made an odd noise in his throat, jerking her torturous thoughts back to the present. "Phillip has become my life."

Darrell felt the truth of his declaration to the marrow of her bones. "He already feels the same about you, Alex."

"Mom?"

Phillip's voice broke the odd tension between them.

"I'm in your bedroom, sweetheart!"

"I heard Dad was back." He came running into the room. "Dad—"

Alex moved to meet him halfway and they hugged.

"Are you free now so we can do something?"

"Not exactly. I brought Isabella with me." Phillip's face fell. "She's waiting to be introduced."

"Is she upset?"

"I think it's more a case of her fearing you won't like her."

"Sure I do. She's going to be your wife."

Phillip had never sounded more mature. He couldn't have said anything guaranteed to please his father more. The fact that Phillip meant it made all the difference.

"Are you hungry, son?" Alex asked in a thick-toned voice.

"Kind of."

"That's good because we're going to meet Isabella in the small dining room downstairs for dinner in a few minutes."

"I've laid out your clothes on the bed," Darrell informed him.

"Okay. I'll hurry."

Alex followed her out of the bedroom into her room. "I've arranged for your dinner to be sent up here."

She turned to face him. "Thank you."

"Darrell—I hope you understand why I didn't include you this evening."

She bit her lip, hoping she hadn't let her disappointment show.

"You don't have to explain. I'm glad I don't have to be there. Phillip will be much more at ease if he's not constantly wondering what I'm thinking. He's his own person and will make his own judgments. I'm sure Isabella will be more comfortable, too. This wouldn't be easy for any woman."

He studied her for a minute. "Thank you for being so unselfish."

Oh, Alex. If you only knew the truth.

"You don't need to thank me. I—I know how important this first meeting is," she stammered. "I'll look forward to getting to know her another time. In fact speaking of time, I'm going to have to get back to my job in Denver pretty soon. So why don't you and Isabella decide what would be best where Phillip is concerned and let me know tomorrow.

"This summer he's enrolled in swimming, tennis and baseball. He'll tell you none of that matters, but I wanted you to know that he has plenty to do if he flies back home with me right away."

Her tongue was starting to run away with her, but she couldn't help it. "The important thing here is that you and Isabella work things out so your wedding goes smoothly. I'll do whatever I can to help."

"I'm ready," Phillip announced, preventing her from hearing Alex's response.

His gaze seemed reluctant to leave hers before he leveled his attention on his son. "I like that blazer."

"Thanks. Will you help me with my tie? I hate them."

"So do I," Alex muttered.

Normally that job was Darrell's domain, but he had a father now, one who performed the task with obvious pleasure.

Darrell winked at Phillip. "You're a sight fit for a king,"

Phillip screwed up his face. "That was corny, Mom."

"I know, but I couldn't help it."

Alex's broad shoulders shook in silent laughter. Their eyes met in shared amusement before he guided Phillip toward the door.

"I hope everything goes well," she called to them.

Phillip hung back. "Aren't you coming?"

"Not this time. I've got a phone call to make so I'll still have a job when I get back to Denver."

"You're not going to lose your job, Mom. Jack told me the

other day he's hoping you'll change your mind and marry him. You've got it made."

"Who's Jack?" Alex asked. By this time they'd crossed over the threshold.

"Mom's boss," came the answer before the door closed.

The click set off a symbolic echo in her heart.

Up to now she'd been focused on Isabella and how hard it was going to be for the princess to have to share Alex with his son.

But watching them walk out of the room just now made Darrell realize she, too, was going to go through a serious adjustment letting Phillip go with his dad.

Darrell had to admit it pained her to be left behind this evening. She was so used to being the center of Phillip's universe, she was actually jealous of Alex's power over him.

Her son's eagerness to go off with his father whether she went with them or not came shouldn't have come as a shock. It was clear they were both anxious to make up for lost time.

That's what she wanted for them! But this was only the beginning. Soon Alex was going to be Isabella's husband… Just imagining it produced excruciating pain of a different kind.

Before Darrell broke down in tears, she showered and changed into a nightgown and robe to have dinner. Once she'd eaten, she realized that too many flying hours had made her desperately tired. Bed called to her.

After brushing her teeth, she doused the lights and turned in, hoping she wouldn't have more disturbing dreams.

Sometime later she thought she heard a noise.

"Phillip?" she called softly in the darkness, too groggy to turn on a light.

"No," came that deep, vibrant male voice.

CHAPTER FIVE

"ALEX—" Suddenly Darrell was wide-awake and sat up. "W-what time is it?"

"Midnight. I'm sorry to have disturbed you. Phillip and I needed to talk. He's asleep now."

She smoothed the hair away from her face. He stood a few feet away from the bed. Anyone looking in right now would be scandalized to see the king in her bedroom. But everything about their situation was unique. Her heart was beating far too fast to be good for her.

"Tell me what happened—"

She heard him exhale. "Our son was such a perfect gentleman, I hardly recognized him."

Since Darrell understood exactly what he meant by that, she didn't misconstrue his words. "He loves you so much, he obviously didn't dare do anything you could fault."

"Isabella wasn't exactly herself, either, though she tried."

"So all in all the evening turned into a disaster," Darrell finished for him.

"That's one way of putting it." But he said it with a chuckle, which in turn caused her to do the same.

"I know it isn't a laughing matter," she said when she'd sobered. "Do you think they liked each other?"

"I think they will once the shock wears off. It's one thing to have intellectual knowledge of each other, and quite another to sit across a table from each other face-to-face for the first time. Everything became real tonight."

Darrell could second that!

She sat up a little straighter. "I'm sure you're thankful this initial meeting is over. Tomorrow it will be easier."

"She's leaving first thing in the morning."

Uh-oh. "Is Phillip upset you're going back to San Ravino with her? If he is, I'll have a talk with him."

"Thank you, but that won't be necessary. She wants to speak to her parents alone, and will send for me when the time is right."

Alarmed, Darrell said, "They don't know yet?"

"She thought it would be better to meet Phillip first."

Darrell put her hands to her face. "It's going to be horrible, isn't it."

"That remains to be seen."

"I feel terrible for her, Alex."

"So do I. Her parents are very decent people. But even decent people have their limits."

Tears trickled out of her eyes. "Do you think Phillip has any idea how important tonight was?"

"Yes." His voice grated. "That's why we talked so long. I heard all about Steve and his divorced parents. We discussed what it was like for his friend to live in two different households with two moms. Our son is much more prepared to deal with this situation than I'd given him credit for."

"He's devoted a lot of thought to it. Too much," Darrell murmured.

"Our son is terrific, but you already know that."

"I do." She wiped the moisture off her cheeks. "We just have to hope Isabella and her parents will be able to work through their pain. Is there any way of putting off the wedding another week or two? Just to give them a little more time to get used to the idea?"

"We talked about that possibility, among others."

"What others?"

"Her parents will probably be able to deal with it as long as Phillip is never allowed to succeed me as king."

"King—" she blurted incredulously. "Phillip?"

Until Alex had brought up the subject just now, the thought had never entered her head. "Did you assure her Phillip is the last person in the world who would want that job one day, let alone be qualified?"

The silence lengthened before he said, "Who knows what's in store for our son." Alex sounded so serious, she started to get nervous.

"I can tell you right now it won't be that!" she cried.

He shifted his weight. "Did I mention his asking me if he was a prince now?"

She made a protesting sound in her throat. "He was just kidding around, Alex. You know how he is. Isabella has nothing to fear from him. When you two have children, they'll be royals from birth. I hope you explained that to him. After I get him alone I'll explain to him."

"Let's not worry about that right now. How would you like to go horseback riding after breakfast in the morning?"

He'd changed the subject too fast.

"I'm sure Phillip will love it."

"Surely you realize I'm including you in the invitation," he said in a voice that brooked no argument.

"Isabella wouldn't approve of it no matter how hard she's trying to be brave about this, so—"

"Be ready at nine," he cut in on her abruptly. "Sleep well."

Within seconds he'd disappeared from the suite.

Shivering with apprehension because the situation was

growing more complicated by the minute, she burrowed under the covers. Five minutes later she was still wide-awake.

Not only their conversation but his presence had given her a serious case of insomnia. The time for gut-wrenching honesty had come.

She hadn't wanted him to leave just now...

Frightened by her feelings for him, which were intensifying beyond her control, she pounded her pillow in an effort to get more comfortable so sleep would come. This insanity had to stop.

One way to cure it would be to leave Switzerland immediately. But how could she do that when nothing had been resolved regarding visitation arrangements?

Just saying the word "visitation" made her cringe.

The thought of leaving her son for any length of time was unbearable.

Yet he'd feel the same way when he had to leave his father.

She wept into her pillow.

What had she done?

Alex had just seen a sober Isabella off at the helipad when his mother phoned, asking him to come by her apartment.

He grimaced. The castle grapevine was alive and doing well.

"Is it true?" she questioned the moment he entered the day room of her suite.

This morning his mother wore a casual dress in a melon tone that suited her light brunette hair. She appeared ready for her daily walk with the two dogs she'd raised from puppies. Since his father's death, they'd brought her a lot of comfort.

He studied her for a long moment. One day soon he intended to tell her the whole truth. But for now the preservation of their family's happiness necessitated his holding back certain information.

"That depends on what you've heard." He kissed her cheek. "If I could have told you sooner, I would have, but Isabella deserved to hear the news before anyone else. She's on her way back to San Ravino as we speak."

Her dark gray eyes looked at him in anguish. "Then it *is* true."

"That I have a twelve-year-old son named Phillip?" He met her gaze head-on. "Yes."

She sank down on the couch, rubbing the dogs' heads absently. "How long have you known?"

"Three days ago Leo came to me with a story about a woman and a ring."

She moaned. "I could expect this from almost anyone else in the world, but not my only son." Her voice shook. "To do this to Isabella…"

Her eyes filled with tears. "How did this happen, Alex? You know what I mean."

He moved toward her. Though he'd braced himself for this inevitable confrontation, it was still difficult to see his mother in pain.

"Chaz and I went to a bar with a couple of girls while we were on vacation in the States. We all drank too much. I only spent one night with her before Chaz and I got word that Uncle Vittorio was in that accident and we had to fly home.

"I don't honestly remember giving her the ring Chaz gave me. When we flew out of Colorado Springs, I knew I wouldn't be back. Nine months later she gave birth to my son, but she had no way of contacting me because she didn't know who I was.

"Phillip has grown up wanting to know his father, so in desperation she used the ring to try to find me."

His mother's expression twisted in agony. "Well, she certainly did that, didn't she."

The dogs moaned at the harsh tone in her voice.

"Every day since your father died, I've asked why he was

taken from us so prematurely. Now I can see it was to spare him this grief." She took a shallow breath. "You've always been so wise, Alex. Whatever possessed you to fly them here, and allow them to stay at the castle?"

"Because he's my son and deserves the very best, despite my irresponsible behavior. He needs love. Isabella understands this and realizes why I refuse to keep him hidden like some bastard child. She knows everything. She had dinner with him last night. We're going to work this out."

Visibly shaken, she got to her feet. "You think for one minute Ernesto and Tatia are going to stand for this?"

His brows furrowed. "Isabella's parents don't have a choice any more than I did."

Her gaze bore into his. "Oh, yes, you did. You could have kept this private, and dealt with him and his mother behind the scene." Leo had suggested the same thing.

"I could have." He folded his arms. "But when you meet Phillip, you'll understand why I didn't."

She shook her head in bewilderment. "Bringing your former lover into our home is political suicide, and so cruel to Isabella I can't imagine what you're thinking."

Though he tried to control it, his temper flared. "Darrell Collier is Phillip's mother, the only parent he's ever known. Would you have me tear him apart from her because of the way it will look to everyone else?"

"You didn't need to bring them here," she reiterated. "It was a grave mistake on your part."

"He's my son, Mother. He needs me, and I…need him."

She shook her head. "I can't believe this has happened."

"I had trouble believing it myself until I met him. He's wonderful. You're going to love him."

His mother looked away. She was trembling.

He moved closer. "The second Darrell came to the castle

asking for an audience with me, Leo did everything he could to keep it quiet, but the rumors began flying anyway. You know as well as I do the best way to handle a situation of this magnitude is to expose it immediately."

"With what results?" Her voice throbbed.

"I don't have the answer to that yet. In this scenario no one set out to hurt anyone, least of all Phillip, who's an innocent. But I *do* know this much. I already love him and want him with me always."

"At the cost of the monarchy?" Her voice rang out. "He can never be your legitimate heir."

Alex struggled to tamp down his anger. "For the sake of argument, why not?"

She let out a cry of alarm. "Because no child of a commoner can inherit the title. It's the law and you know it."

"Laws can be changed."

"Then you'd be the first Valleder king in over a thousand years to do away with it."

"You have to admit it's archaic."

Their eyes held while she digested his blunt honesty. "But you wouldn't change it."

He took a fortifying breath. "No, Mother. I wouldn't."

Until he saw that steely look enter her eyes, he thought his answer had satisfied her. She stared at him like she'd never seen him before.

"This isn't as much about your son as the woman who gave birth to him. Something tells me you never got over her. Why else would you give her a ring that could be traced? It explains your irrational decision to put her in the Saxony apartment. No wonder you've kept putting off your marriage to Isabella."

"Stop, Mother. You're wrong you know."

She shook her head. "No, I'm not. The maid told me she's

blond and enchantingly beautiful in that special American way. She wears no wedding ring.

"How shrewd of her to come forward weeks before your wedding and present you with the fruit of your passion, knowing the twelve-year-old son of her body would blind you to your royal duty."

"Mother— There are things you don't know."

"I'm not blind, deaf and dumb, Alex." Her voice trembled. "I know you're not in love with Isabella and never have been. But I thought—I hoped that with marriage and children, love would come the way it did with your father and me."

"I'm hoping for that, too," he declared. At least he'd always held that hope, but Darrell's sudden advent into his life had knocked him sideways. The more he was around her, the more he wanted to be around her all the time. If the truth be known, he *wanted* her. It was a fact he could no longer deny.

She shook her head. "What you've done is make it almost impossible for that to happen now. Not with that woman back in your life!"

His mother was right. No one knew that better than Alex.

"Ms. Collier has no shame, no decency. To think you lost your heart to such a person pains me as much as your father's death."

Alex ground his teeth. "Before you jump to any more erroneous conclusions, I'm going to ask a favor of you. This is important." He checked his watch.

"I'm due to take Phillip riding right now. During your walk with the dogs, why don't you pass by the stables in say three hours. That way your first meeting with him will be informal and spontaneous, putting him at ease. Later on in the day you and I will have another private talk."

Her expression remained wooden. "Are you asking as the king, or as my son?"

"Both. I swear on father's grave that if you'll do this,

certain things will become clear and help you get through this without completely despising me."

At the mention of his father, she lowered her head. That was the way he left her as he slipped out of the apartment. At their next meeting he would tell her about Melissa. By that time she would have come face-to-face with her grandson.

Knowing his mother as he did, her heart would soften. She'd want Phillip to stay in Bris and become an intrinsic part of the family. Once that happened, she wouldn't be able to dismiss Phillip's second mother so easily...

A steep hill rose beyond the lake bordering the back of the royal estate. It led to vineyards and ultimately the forested slopes of the mountains overlooking the magnificent Rhine Valley.

By the time the three of them dismounted to rest and take in the view, euphoria had overtaken Darrell.

During the climb, Alex had put Phillip to work checking the riverbank for signs of dead fish, which he explained was a problem in the lower Ungadine called Whirling disease. His minister of fisheries was working with some biologists to eradicate it.

Phillip thought the term "whirling" was too funny, but he took his father's suggestion seriously. Already Alex was making his son feel important. He managed him without dictating. Phillip had never been more pleasant or well behaved.

While she wandered around stretching her legs, Alex tied up the horses. She hadn't ridden one in years. At the end of the day she would be sore, but the glorious ride had been worth it.

Phillip didn't seem to have the same problem, lucky boy.

"Dad? Have you ever climbed up to that ridge?"

"Many times."

"With my grandpa?"

"No. He was always too busy."

"How come he was so mean?"

"Not mean, Phillip. It's just that when he pledged to serve the people of our country, he meant it. You have to understand he represented the House of Valleder. It has reigned over this canton for centuries.

"The castle here in Bris has been our ancestral home since the Middle Ages. Father never forgot his duty for a minute."

Darrell could hear her son's mind taking it all in.

"How long was he king?"

"Thirty years before he died of a heart attack."

"I bet you miss him a lot."

"The whole family does."

Following his father's soulful remark Phillip eyed him with a distinct glint.

"What do you bet I can climb to the top of that ridge and back in half an hour."

"I used to make that trip in twenty minutes," Alex said with a deadpan expression.

Phillip let out a whoop. "You're on!" He high-fived his dad before taking off. Pretty soon he'd disappeared in the pines.

Alex put a booted foot on the log, turning to Darrell with one of those white smiles that melted her insides.

He looked happy.

In jeans and a navy pullover, he was jaw-dropping gorgeous.

There wasn't another man to equal him.

This must have been the way Melissa felt when she'd gone to that bar with him years ago. No woman would be able to resist an invitation to join him in his sleeping bag. Darrell took back everything she'd ever said to her sister about not having shown more sense.

"I'm sure it isn't really possible to imagine your life if you weren't raised to be a king, but I'm curious to know what you think you might have done with your life if you'd been born as say…Alex Smith."

He leaned on his knee with one arm. "That's easy to answer. I would have worked in counterespionage developing various codes no enemy could crack."

"How fascinating! I remember the story of the Wind Talkers who were Navajo military men used during the war. No one could break their code."

"Exactly. We speak a lot of languages here in Switzerland, and each one has its different dialects depending on the region or valley. The Romanche dialects are complex and fascinating to me, as is the Navajo language you were referring to."

"Phillip has a lot to learn."

"Hopefully he'll want to. Our language will be lost if we don't endeavor to keep it unified and used. When I wasn't busy with some regimen or other, I began making my own dictionary of Romanche words and idioms, incorporating the dialects.

"On mountain hikes I always carry a notebook with me in case I meet a fellow countryman who could give me a new word here or there to add to my collection."

"You're a very brilliant man. Phillip's in awe of you."

"My father was the brilliant one," he informed her. "He was first to introduce a program at the university in Bris to get as much information as we can from the old people still living within the canton. Once they're gone, any knowledge they have will die with them. I'd hate to see Romanche go by the wayside."

"Thank goodness for a sovereign like you who cares enough to preserve your heritage," she said emotionally.

He moved closer to her. "The main reason I spent time in Arizona was to visit some Navajo reservations and see how they preserve their dialects and gather information. But I must admit the idea of being a secret agent has headed the top of my list for a profession."

His eyes narrowed on her face. "What about you? If there'd been no Phillip, what would you have done?"

"That's an easy question to answer, too. My grandmother never did have very good health. I probably would have tried to get into medical school somewhere. Maybe become an internist. But like you, I had other responsibilities that pretty well grounded me to one place and one priority."

"I'm assuming you're the one who chose to stay home with your grandmother while your sister went to work at the dude ranch."

"Yes, but in all fairness to Melissa, she waited on my grandmother, too. Though I worried about her, I was glad she could get away to do something she thought would be fun. Her best friend's uncle had horses, so she went riding a lot. The dude ranch was the perfect place for her, and it paid a good salary."

But Melissa had ended up taking on more than she could handle when she'd met Alex.

Darrell wouldn't have been able to forget him, either. Her desire for him had already become so acute, it was a full-grown pain only he could assuage. Yet to even entertain thoughts of him was taboo.

A relationship with the king of Valleder wasn't possible, not on any level. Melissa's brief interlude with him had been one of those fantastic accidents in life that had defied the odds.

To stand around alone with him any longer pretending she didn't have feelings for him wasn't only ridiculous, it was unbearable. Finally she made the decision to separate herself from him. There was only one way to do it.

After loosening the reins around the tree trunk, she climbed back on the surefooted mare Alex had chosen for her.

In a few swift strides he closed in on her. "What do you think you're doing?"

"I'm going to see if I can beat you and Phillip back to the stable."

His features tautened visibly. "Why?"

Don't ask me that question.

"Our son loves competition. For once I'd like to be the one to give him a run for his money."

"Surely not at the expense of a broken neck."

She frowned. "Am I such a lame rider?"

"Anyone can have an accident. While you're my guest, I prefer to keep you safe."

So saying he reached for her, pulling her off the horse before she was ready.

The momentum brought their bodies together. Helplessly she slid down his powerful physique until her feet touched the ground.

The incredible sensation caused a gasp to escape her lips. Their eyes met by accident. His blazed a hot green.

"Alex—" she whispered mindlessly, caught in a sensuous thrall where the world seemed far removed from them at this moment.

An answering moan came from his throat before his mouth closed over hers with a kind of refined savagery she would never have suspected.

She kept telling herself this couldn't be happening. Not possibly.

Like a drowning person going under for the third time, her life flashed before her. She thought of all the reasons why this was wrong—out of the question…

He was going to be a married man within a few weeks.

But the rightness of being in his arms, the feeling that they were two halves of a whole transcended every moral objection. Fused to him like this, everything changed.

She didn't need his hand at her waist crushing her to him

because she molded herself to him of her own free will, wanting to merge with him.

His other hand cradled the back of her head, the better for their mouths to savor the intoxicating elixir while they slowly began to devour each other. Their mutual hunger wasn't some vain imagination. It was a kind of craving she'd never known in her life, like a force beyond herself that wanted, needed everything this man had to give.

Every kiss he gave her went deeper and longer, driving her wild with desire. The increasing urgency of his demand set off an explosion of need inside her.

Feverish with longings her arms slid around his waist and she found herself melded to every hard line and sinew. All she kept praying was don't stop this ecstasy, don't ever stop.

Her legs grew heavy. Her palms throbbed with pains brought on by too much pleasure. His mouth was driving her mad with the things he was doing to her.

"I'm back!" shouted a voice in the distance.

Both of them groaned before she cried, "What if he's seen us?" In panic Darrell tore her lips from his and jerked away from those strong arms holding her possessively.

The motion made her dizzy. He steadied her swaying motion.

"Are you all right?" he whispered.

"Y-yes. You go to him."

Alex's recovery was much faster than hers. He moved toward Phillip, giving her a chance to gain her equilibrium behind the protection of the tree. By the time they'd joined her, Darrell was astride her horse ready to go back.

She was still so shaken by what had transpired, she struggled to pretend nothing was wrong. "Did you make it in ten minutes?" she forced herself to ask Phillip.

"No, but I will next time."

"Eleven and a half minutes isn't bad for your first time."

Alex tousled Phillip's hair. "Now we'd better go. I've discovered I'm hungry for lunch."

Heat enveloped her.

"Me, too," Phillip declared.

After they'd climbed on their horses, she trailed them down the mountain. Phillip did most of the talking. He couldn't fathom that Bris was a four-thousand-year-old city built by the Romans. It was a good thing he was so eager to learn from his father. It prevented him from noticing how quiet she'd become.

Little did her son know her emotions were in utter chaos.

A line had been crossed today.

She didn't have the power to turn back time to prevent the experience from happening. However she could make certain there would never be a repeat.

There was no excuse for losing her head. Until he'd admitted that he hadn't been emotionally involved with Melissa, she would have assumed he'd lost his because she reminded him of her sister. Though the two of them had different coloring, physically they resembled each other in many ways.

Darrell could have understood him getting caught off guard in a small detour down memory lane, but according to him he couldn't even remember that night with Melissa clearly. So what was the explanation?

Certainly it was a mistake! One of those heart-stopping, forbidden mistakes of unmatchable rapture she would remember for the rest of her life.

Deep in agonizing thought she scarcely remembered the ride back to the stable. Once she'd walked outside the barn, she caught sight of a cute, dark blond boy running toward Alex. He was calling out something to him in Romanche.

"Speak English, Jules."

The boy reminded her of Phillip when he'd been a few years younger. They all bore that distinguishing Valleder stamp.

Alex put his hand on the boy's shoulder. "Where's Vito?"

"Around the front with Aunt Katerina."

He guided him closer. "Jules? I'd like you to meet a relative from Colorado in the United States. I hope you'll all become good friends."

Jules looked up at Alex in surprise. "I didn't know we had relatives in America."

"You have *one*. His name is Phillip. He's my son."

The boy's light blue eyes rounded in disbelief. "No, he's not—"

For Darrell it was déjà vu because Phillip had sounded exactly like that when she'd told him his father was the king. The two boys had so much in common it was uncanny.

"Freaky, huh," Phillip spoke up.

Alex smiled at his son. "Jules doesn't know what freaky means."

"Crazy."

Jules was understandably bewildered. "How old are you?"

"Almost thirteen."

Going on a hundred, Darrell muttered inwardly. Alex flashed her an amused glance as if he'd just thought the same thing. Her heart lurched every time he looked at her.

"Isabella's not your mother," Jules declared.

"No," Darrell interjected, trying to ignore Alex. "*I* am. My name is Darrell Collier. I'm very pleased to meet you, Jules." She put out her hand, which he shook politely. But it was clear he was puzzled.

Who wouldn't be? The poor boy didn't know Melissa had given birth to Phillip. But this was hardly the time and place for Darrell or Alex to get into the specifics.

Unfortunately it left the impression that Darrell and Alex had been lovers. One day soon the truth would come out. In the meantime she had to withstand Jules's curiosity.

He finally switched his gaze back to Alex. "Then how come you're going to marry Isabella?"

Darrell had anticipated his question and was ready for it. "Because she's a royal princess and they love each other very much."

"Isabella's really cool," Phillip piped up.

Jules glanced back at his new relative in fascination. "What does cool mean?"

"She's a fox."

Well, well, well. If her son said it, it meant Isabella was a true beauty.

Of course she would be, but the knowledge acted like a dagger plunged in Darrell's heart.

"A fox?" Jules questioned.

Alex burst into laughter.

Jules looked so worn-out trying to figure everything out, Darrell took pity on him.

"What Phillip's trying to say is that Isabella is a lovely person."

Those light blue eyes studied her, then Phillip. "Do you want to come and see Great-Aunt Katerina's dogs?"

"Sure. What kind are they?"

Jules looked to Alex for the answer.

"In English they're called golden retrievers. Stick with my son, Jules, and your English vocabulary is going to skyrocket."

"Go on with him," Darrell urged Phillip. "I'm going back for a soak in the tub."

He grinned. "You didn't do half bad on that horse, Mom."

"Thanks a lot, *Roy*."

Her allusion to Roy Rogers, the famous cowboy, would be lost on Jules, but Alex and Phillip laughed.

"Come on, Dad."

She felt Alex's gaze compelling her to look at him, but that was all over. She didn't dare allow herself another second alone with him. She didn't want a postmortem of what had happened up on the mountain. Until Alex and Isabella sorted things out in the next couple of days, she intended to stay sequestered in the apartment away from everyone.

Turning on her heel, she took a path through the trees that would lead back to the castle without her having to see Alex's mother.

One day they would have to meet, but not right now. Not while the feel and taste of her son's hands and mouth had rocked Darrell's world.

CHAPTER SIX

ALEX left Phillip and the boys in his mother's apartment. She'd invited all of them to lunch. Knowing they'd be occupied several hours at least, he slipped out to take the inevitable phone call from Isabella.

Her parents expected him for dinner. That gave him three hours to talk to Darrell before the helicopter took off.

He had an idea she'd barricaded herself in the suite. The passion they'd shared had not only scared the daylights out of her, but it had changed him into someone he didn't know anymore.

He took the stairs down to the second floor and walked through the hallway until he reached her door. Before he knocked, he pulled out his cell phone to call her.

There was no answer, however he hadn't expected her to pick up.

He knew instinctively she was hiding from him. Maybe she would answer the door if he knocked, thinking it was the maid. But there was no response—no sound to indicate she was inside.

In his gut he knew she'd made up her mind not to open it, not even for the king.

But the *man* could gain access to her without anyone knowing about it—the man Alex had been repressing since that wild night years ago—the man who seemed to have been reborn since discovering he had a son...

The only way to do this meant going through the music room on the first floor located directly below the Saxony apartment. The rope Chaz had attached from the balcony to reach both floors still hung outside the window.

Driven by a need he could no longer control, Alex went downstairs and stole inside the room past the grand piano. He opened the window to test the rope's strength, figuring it would still hold him. If it didn't, he'd fall in the lake. It had happened many times before without incident.

After getting out on the ledge, he grasped the thick cord and started climbing hand over hand.

It wasn't as easy as it used to be. The years had taken a toll on his athletic prowess. If Chaz saw him now, he'd laugh his head off.

One more burst of energy and he would be home free.

"Darrell Collier?" he called out to her. "I'm coming up to you so be warned!"

In the next instant he heard an answering scream. Luckily the thick castle walls would have muted her cry.

"I hope you're presentable because I'm almost there. We have to talk."

He threw his arm over the balcony wall and hoisted himself so only his head and shoulders were visible.

She stood there clutching the lapels of her robe to her throat. "Are you out of your mind, Alex?"

He could read several emotions coming from those violet eyes, but the dominant one was fear for his safety.

"That all depends on your definition," he drawled.

She stamped her foot impatiently. "You're going to fall!"

"It wouldn't be the first time."

"Be serious," she begged. Her face had gone pale.

"I've never been more serious in my life. I have to fly to Italy in a little while, so I won't be able to see you or Phillip until tomorrow."

Her appealing body was trembling. "You could have phoned me with that information."

"I tried. When that didn't work I knocked on your door."

She bit her lip. "I—I was asleep."

"Here at the window you mean?"

Suddenly her color came flooding back into her cheeks. "This isn't funny, Alex. You could plunge to your death. Please come inside," she implored him.

"You're sure? I wouldn't want you accusing me of taking advantage of you."

"Yes, I'm sure!" she practically shouted at him.

"Since you asked me so nicely, I think I will."

Another lunge brought him within a foot of her. She backed away like a frightened fawn in the forest.

She had every right to be nervous of him. At the moment he was feeling invincible. But it was the wrong decade, the wrong country, the wrong woman.

"I'm not going to apologize for kissing you today. I thoroughly enjoyed it. You're a beautiful woman. It was one of those incredible summer mornings, and I couldn't resist.

"That's no excuse, but it's the best explanation I can offer. As long as I'm engaged to Isabella, I swear it won't happen again. That's what I came to say. I want you to be able to trust me. If we don't have that, we don't have anything."

"I agree." Her voice caught. "What happened was both our faults. Of course I trust you. I think the situation with Phillip threw us, but no longer."

Phillip had nothing to do with the chemistry between them, Alex reasoned to himself. But he decided to let her remark pass because he had tangible proof she desired him, too. She could deny it all she wanted, but the fact remained they were both on fire for each other with no help in sight.

"You sound totally recovered."

"I am," she assured him. After pausing for breath she asked, "Where's Phillip now?"

"With mother and the boys. Though she's not ready to admit it yet, she's having the time of her life getting to know her grandson. The boys are in shock. The reality of Phillip has already shaken Vito out of his morose state. As for Jules, he's just plain delighted with his upstart cousin from across the Atlantic."

Her mouth curved upward, bewitching him. "Upstart is right."

"Darrell—" he said before she could say anything else. "I know how hard the situation is on you. I don't expect you to remain in this limbo forever. Just give me until tomorrow. After being with Isabella, I'll know a lot more."

She nodded. "It's all right. I checked with Jack. He told me to use this time for my vacation."

Alex's hands curled into fists. No doubt *Jack* was counting the hours until she flew back. What a fool her boss was to let her out of his sight.

"Is there anything I can do for you before I leave? Anything at all?"

She shook her gilt-blond head without looking at him. "I feel like I'm living in a dream. How could I possibly want anything more?"

How indeed.

"I'll be in touch with you in the morning and we'll go from there. Do me a favor and answer the phone so I don't have to risk my life a second time in order to have a conversation with you?"

She lifted anxious eyes to him. "I'm sorry. I promise to answer it."

Before he proved that he couldn't keep a promise to her five minutes, let alone a lifetime, he slipped back over the side of the balcony.

"Alex—"

She sounded terrified for him, but he kept on going, not daring to let her cries stop him or heaven help them both.

When he'd swung himself back inside the music room and had locked the window, he phoned the palace security guard out in the hall. "There's a rope hanging from the balcony of the Saxony apartment to the outside of the music room. It's a security risk and needs to be removed ASAP."

"I thought you didn't want it cut down."

"I've changed my mind." I don't trust myself anymore.

"Yes, Your Majesty."

"Mom?"

"Hi, sweetheart!"

"Jules and Vito are with me."

Glad she was showered and dressed in a blouse and skirt, she hurried into the drawing room of their apartment. The ten-year-old Vito looked like the rest of them. With so many similarities, they could all be brothers. It really was remarkable.

"You're Vito. I'm so happy to meet you."

"Hello, Ms. Collier."

"Call her Darrell," Phillip told him.

While they shook hands his darker blue eyes studied her with interest. "Jules and I have to go to the dentist. We're going shopping, too. Can Phillip come with us? Mother says it's okay. We'll walk him back after dinner."

She looked at Phillip. "Would you like to go?"

"Since Dad's not here, sure."

"Then it's fine with me." She looked at the boys. "Tell your mother thank you."

"I will," Vito replied, sounding too grown up for his age.

As they started to leave she heard Jules say, "You're lucky. Nobody ever gets to stay in this apartment."

"Why not?"

"We don't know. Mother says it's a secret," Jules explained.

"Why don't you just ask Dad?"

Vito shook his head. "Mother said it wasn't our business."

"Then I'll ask him when he gets back from Italy."

Darrell thought she heard the word "cool" come from Jules before the outer door closed.

She walked around the room, stopping to smell the gorgeous white roses that gave off a heavenly perfume.

Not even Isabella had slept in here?

Whatever the reason, Alex had taken Phillip to his heart, breaking rules only a king could do if he wanted to.

He'd risked causing what could be an insurmountable problem in his coming marriage to the princess in order to claim him and make up for the last twelve years.

A man like that didn't come along very often in life. Isabella could have no conception of how lucky she was.

Before Darrell fell apart over her feelings for Alex, she phoned Rudy and asked him to have a car waiting for her. There was a famous art gallery in the center of the main shopping district she wanted to visit. Anything to get her mind off of Alex, who would be spending tonight with Isabella. The images of the two of them entwined together while he convinced her their marriage would work made Darrell writhe in pain.

She grabbed her purse and flew out of the apartment. If her bodyguard thought she was having some kind of nervous breakdown, he'd be right!

Alex had just finished shaving when his cell phone rang. He checked the caller ID and clicked on. "Mother?"

"I'm on my way to your apartment. You can't leave for San Ravino until we've talked." The line went dead.

He rushed to get dressed. By the time he'd shrugged into his suit jacket, she was at the door. The dogs preceded her into his living room. After shutting the door he leaned against it, waiting…

"Oh, Alex—he's so much like you when you were that age, I can hardly believe it!" There were tears in her voice as well as her eyes.

Gratified by her response, he drew in a deep breath and walked toward her. "I see you and father in him, too. And Chaz…"

She nodded. "Yes. He has a way of expressing himself like your cousin. He and the boys could be brothers."

"So now you know why I had to bring him with me."

"*I* understand it," she whispered, "but your uncle won't."

He tautened. "We can thank God Uncle Vittorio and Aunt Renate are away on a trip. I agree he would go into a black rage knowing what happened on that vacation in Colorado years ago.

"Perhaps now you understand why it was imperative I announced paternity before their return from the cruise."

His mother stared at him while streams of unspoken thoughts passed between them. "Yes," she eventually agreed in an unsteady voice. Her wet eyes gazed at him for a long time. "But you might have done it to the peril of the monarchy."

Lines darkened his face. "I love Phillip."

She let out a weary sigh. "How could you not? But you can't expect Isabella to take him to her heart."

He grasped her hands. "She's making a gallant effort."

His mother shuddered. "I can't imagine how she's going to get past this, Alex. It's not just the reality of Phillip. You brought his mother with you. How painful for Isabella to have to live with the fact that you were intimate with the woman staying under our roof."

He let go of her hands to rub his chin where he'd nicked himself with the razor. "It's asking a lot of Isabella, but so far she's handling it. I'll find out how well when I see her tonight." After checking his watch he said, "I have to go."

"Wait—"

His gaze swung back to hers. "What is it?"

"Since Ms. Collier is Phillip's mother and has worked her way into the castle, how do you know she won't make trouble for you and Isabella?"

Alex had been waiting for that salvo. "If that had been her intention, she would have surfaced years ago instead of this week. Even then she couldn't go through with telling me I had a son. I had to fly to Colorado in order to pry it out of her.

"At that point she still begged me not to act on the knowledge. When I brought her and Phillip back with me, she asked me again to turn the plane around because she knew what would happen if I didn't.

"Darrell is still suffering over it. If you knew her as I already do, she's frightened of hurting Isabella, so you don't have to worry about her causing problems."

"Listen to you defend her!" Her voice shook. "She's gotten to you the way she did once before. You were obviously so taken with her, you gave her the ring your cousin had made specially for you. Now that she's found you, she has decided to enamor you all over again."

Darrell didn't have to try. Whatever had driven them into each other's arms today, it hadn't been planned, not on either of their parts. His heart almost failed him remembering the lushness of her avid mouth opening to the pressure of his.

"By claiming Phillip so readily, you've allowed her to

believe anything's possible!" his mother exclaimed. "The more I hear about this woman, the more I don't trust her."

He moved to the door, then looked back at her. "If I didn't know something you still don't know, I wouldn't trust her, either."

"What more could there be?"

It was time for the whole truth.

"Phillip's birth mother was named *Melissa* Collier."

That caught his mother's attention in a hurry.

"She died of an aneurism after giving birth to Phillip. Her sister, Darrell, adopted him. The only reason Darrell came looking for me was to help her unhappy son and honor her sister's dying wish that he get to know his father.

"In point of fact, Darrell had no prior knowledge of my existence until two weeks ago when she had the ring traced and saw a picture of me on the Internet. She noticed the strong resemblance to Phillip and jumped to the only conclusion she could.

"Therefore you're going to have to reassess your thinking about her. She has no designs on the man who impregnated her sister." In fact she had every reason to despise him, which made what happened up in the mountains even more remarkable.

If ever anyone looked shell-shocked, it was his mother. "This is unbelievable."

"But true. And you have to admit Darrell's done an amazing job of raising her sister's son."

His mother made a cry like she'd been mortally wounded. "I'll grant you he's a fine boy, but what you've just told me alarms me even more."

"Why?"

"Because I can tell this woman means something to you. I can *feel* it!"

She wasn't his mother for nothing.

"I admit I admire her." He wished that was all he felt for her. "Darrell was only in her teens when Melissa died. Since then she has sacrificed her life for Phillip. She could have put him up for adoption instead of adopting him herself. She's made the perfect home for him. He's bright, talented."

A frantic look crossed over his mother's face. "Does Isabella know he was adopted? Does she realize Ms. Collier isn't his real mother?"

His lips thinned. "Not yet. If she agrees to marry me, I'll tell her the truth on our honeymoon. Hopefully the news that Darrell and I were never involved will relieve her fears.

"But for now, no one but you and Phillip know the truth. I don't want Phillip hurt by this.

"Make no mistake—" His body went rigid. "Darrell's his real mother. It was her eyes he first saw when he came into the world."

The most fabulous eyes Alex had ever seen. Like the rare violet hue of the morning sky silhouetting the peaks of the Alps.

"You know what I meant—"

He opened the door. "I don't have time for this now, Mother. Isabella and her parents are waiting for me."

The whirr of the helicopter's rotors sounded overhead. Phillip and the boys ran into Darrell's room to look at it from the balcony.

"Dad's back! We're going to go meet him.'

"Wait, Phillip—" Darrell cautioned.

"Why?"

"Because he always has important things to do first."

"That's what mother says," Jules muttered. Vito nodded. They adored Alex, but they also revered him as king. Phillip had a different problem. To him Alex was his father. Period.

"He said he'd phone you when he could, sweetheart."

"But it's already afternoon."

Darrell was painfully aware he was long overdue. He and Isabella must have managed to work things out, otherwise he would probably have come home a lot sooner.

In order to pass the time without falling apart, she'd talked Phillip into taking a walk on the extensive grounds with her. Then they'd gone swimming with the boys.

The four of them would still be having fun if clouds hadn't started to gather. At the first sign of lightning she'd insisted they go indoors. A storm was almost upon them. Darrell was thankful the helicopter had landed before Alex got caught in the downpour.

She shivered when she remembered his cousin's plane had gone down in bad weather, leaving his sons fatherless.

They were so darling, Darrell couldn't help but love them. She could tell Phillip liked them, too. It was a heady experience to be looked up to by the younger princes who were already enriching his life.

Alex had been worried about Phillip not wanting to hang around waiting to spend time with him. But his fears were groundless. You couldn't separate Phillip from his father now or ever.

"I'll get it," Phillip called out the second the phone rang.

Darrell's heart raced so hard it was a good thing he picked up instead of her. Since he'd climbed up her balcony, the less she had to interact with Alex the better.

Their conversation didn't last long. Phillip hung up and turned to her with an excited look on his face.

"Dad wants us to meet him at his office. He says he's got something special planned and you have to come, too, Mom, because we're going to have dinner with Aunt Evelyn after."

Aunt Evelyn…

Darrell hadn't even met the boys' mother yet, but Phillip was already calling her aunt.

"Hurrah!" Jules cried enthusiastically.

Under the circumstances Darrell couldn't refuse. It was a good thing she'd put on her pleated tan pants and fitted purple top. Not too dressy, not too casual for her first meeting with his cousin-in-law.

The boys knew their way around the castle blindfolded. She followed them down the exquisitely sculpted marble staircase to the first floor. They took a right through the magnificent vaulted corridors lined with paintings and tapestries leading to the king's official workplace.

"See the flag?" Vito spoke up.

"Yes."

"If the Valleder flag is posted, then you know Uncle Alex is in the city and his ministers can have access to him."

"That's very interesting. Thank you for telling me."

"You're welcome."

The boy knew everything and took it all so seriously, Darrell decided he had the makings of a king.

Then she glimpsed the real king. At the first sight of Alex in a black turtleneck and jeans standing in the huge double doorway, her pulse skittered off the charts.

The boys huddled around him while he gave their dark blond heads a gentle roughing.

Yesterday she'd felt those strong hands in her hair and knew how it felt. She almost passed out reliving the sensation until she remembered he'd spent the night with Isabella.

Judging by his laid-back demeanor, he'd won Isabella over and there was going to be a wedding. Then she would always have the right to his affection.

Darrell couldn't bear it.

"Mom?" Phillip shook her arm, jerking her from a place

she'd promised herself never to go again. Her gaze happened to collide with a penetrating pair of eyes that were more gray than green at the moment.

"When a storm rages, there's a knight whose ghost walks around the castle below the waterline. Chaz and I only saw the back of him one time. I thought we'd all go down and search for him now."

The boys laughed nervously. Phillip smiled, but his heels moved up and down, indicating his adrenaline had kicked in.

"Think you're up to it?"

Alex had issued her a direct challenge she couldn't refuse. In truth she didn't want to. Who else besides Alex would think up something this entertaining for a bunch of adventurous boys on a dark, dreary afternoon inside a castle of all things?

"I wouldn't miss snooping around this place for anything in the world."

Another smile of satisfaction curved his lips. "Then let's go."

With a heavy-duty flashlight in hand, Alex strode down the hall forcing everyone to run after him.

"Admit you're a little freaked, Mom."

She was, but not for the reason her son was suggesting.

Alex led them down another hall and through a heavy wooden door to the ancient part of the castle. A circular stone staircase over a thousand years old seemed to go down, down forever. The only light came from the slit windows spaced every so often. Rain beat against the panes.

Without the flashlight they would have been entombed in total darkness once they reached the bottom.

Alex flashed the beam around the vast cavern with its labyrinths and pillars. Water dripped from the dank walls where moss was growing. Above them she could hear the waves on the lake crashing against the castle walls. It caused her to shiver.

"Whoa—" Phillip whispered. Vito stood manfully by himself, but Jules stuck close to his uncle.

"Stay with me everybody," Alex warned them. They advanced a few feet.

"What are those chains for?" Jules asked.

Darrell could see them lying on the stone floor at the base of one of the pillars.

"When it's good weather, the knight is the castle's prisoner."

"No, he's not, Dad—"

"Shh. I think I can hear him," Alex whispered. He handed Phillip the flashlight. "Go ahead with the boys. See what you can find."

"Come on you guys. Dad's only teasing us."

Strange how the darkness made Alex stand out to Darrell as if it were full daylight. She could feel the warmth from his body though they weren't touching. She knew he was smiling.

"I take it you and your cousin used to come down here to play."

"All the time."

"Did your parents know?"

"Not if we could help it. Security wasn't as tight back then, so we got away with a lot."

"Your son appears to be fearless. You couldn't have planned anything more thrilling than this. He's going to want to bring his friends down here when they come to visit."

The second the words left her mouth, she realized her mistake. "I shouldn't have said that. I apologize."

"For what?" The air sizzled with tension.

"For assuming that everything's normal when I know it's anything but. I—I've been thinking about you and Isabella. The only way your marriage can work is for us to set up a visitation schedule that will make her happy.

"Phillip knows exactly what's at stake here. He might not

like it, but now that he feels your love he'll be able to plan his life around the times when he can see you. It'll work. Maybe next time he can bring his friend Ryan."

She heard the changed tenor of his breathing. "Of course his friends will always be welcome, but I want him around more than two or three times a year, Darrell. I want you to move to Bris."

Her heart slammed into her ribs. "You couldn't mean permanently."

"Is that so hard to understand? It would solve a lot of problems."

For you and our son, Alex. Not for me or the princess or the monarchy.

"I couldn't do that. My life's in Denver. Yours is with Isabella and the family you're going to raise. After your wedding is over and things have settled down for you, Phillip can fly here to see you. As long as he can talk to you on the phone between trips, it'll be fine."

Sucking in her breath she added, "It's awfully chilly down here. I think I'll wait for all of you upstairs."

Relying on her instincts to guide her, she turned back toward the staircase, needing to get away from him before she found herself considering his wishes.

To her dismay she stumbled into the bottom step. But the cry she emitted came from the feel of Alex's hands on her hips. At the first touch she longed for him to turn her in his arms and kiss her as if they had the right to lose themselves in each other.

But he belonged to someone else and she needed to get far away and stay there.

"Did you hurt yourself?" He'd asked the question out of concern, but the way his hands slid up her arms before relinquishing her body told her he hadn't forgotten yesterday's incident. The one she hadn't been able to dismiss from her memory no matter how hard she tried.

"No—I'm all right, thank you."

Frightened by her weakness for him, she began the long circular climb, knowing he couldn't come after her while the boys were still down there.

By the time she reached the top, to her surprise the rest of them weren't far behind her. They filed into the lighted hallway.

"Mom? I didn't think you'd get scared down there."

"I didn't, either." Her voice shook.

But being alone with Alex for any reason was too dangerous now. A few minutes ago she'd been willing to crush him in her arms and be swept away again by the passion that had flared between them on the mountain.

She addressed Jules. "Did you see the ghost?"

"No, but we heard something."

"It was a rat," Vito informed him. Darrell cringed.

"Maybe next time," Alex muttered, taking the flashlight from Phillip. "It looks like the worst of the storm has passed over. Let's hurry home to your mom. I bet she's fixed her homemade Wiener schnitzel for us."

The last thing Darrell felt like doing was meeting the boys' mother. She was too shaken up by what had happened in the dark.

To have lost control yesterday was one thing. To almost lose control again today was something else. She hadn't imagined Alex's low moan once his hands had molded to her body. Desire had engulfed both of them.

Maybe it was because he represented forbidden fruit that she trembled even thinking about him.

Possibly the fact that she was forbidden fruit produced a similar response in him.

This close to the wedding you'd have thought just the opposite would be true.

Maybe this was Alex's own sort of private bachelor party—

a kind of midnight-hour urge to let go before he became a married man.

That explanation made the most sense to Darrell.

It was kind of like his princely lapse with Melissa years ago. Only her sister hadn't had the sense to run from the fire.

Apparently the Collier women were pushovers, but Darrell was putting an end to it right now.

CHAPTER SEVEN

"Do YOU know going down those steps made me a little dizzy?" Darrell said loud enough for everyone to hear. "I need to rest for a while. Will you please tell Evelyn how sorry I am? We'll meet another time."

"It made me kind of dizzy, too," Jules piped up. Bless his heart.

Alex herded them along the hallway. "Go ahead with the boys, Phillip. I'll see your mom to the apartment, then I'll come."

No!

"Actually, Alex, I'd like Phillip to come with me."

Maybe it was the tone in her voice. Whatever the explanation, for once Alex didn't insist and her son didn't fight her.

"Sure, Mom. You don't look very good."

"If I feel better later, we'll walk over."

The boys acted disappointed. She didn't dare glance at Alex.

Shifting around she headed toward the center staircase.

It seemed to take forever until she could hurry up the steps and down the hall to their apartment. Phillip followed her inside and shut the door.

She went on through to her bedroom. After slipping off her sandals, she lay down on the bed, curling up on her side.

Phillip sat next to her. "You don't like Dad, huh."

She threw her arm over her eyes. What he'd just said was better than hearing "You're in love with him, huh." But neither version was satisfactory.

"What makes you say that, sweetheart?"

"You never want to be around him. I know it's because he hurt my real mother. But he didn't *try* to hurt her."

Darrell was his real mother, but she knew what he meant.

"I don't dislike him, Phillip. I've come to realize he's a wonderful man."

"Then how come you're mean to him?"

She raised her head to look at him. "Mean?"

"Yeah. He does all these neat things and you always want to stay in here."

Good heavens.

"That's so the two of you can have time together alone."

"But he wants you to do everything with us."

"He said that?"

"No. But I can tell. Remember at the house when he said he didn't blame me for hating him?"

"Yes?"

"Well I think he thinks you still hate him."

Phillip had it all wrong, but she couldn't tell him the truth.

Another troubled sigh came out of him. "Even if you don't like him, can't you try to be nicer?"

If only Phillip knew the truth. Thank goodness he didn't!

"Of course, sweetheart."

"Thanks." After a minute he asked, "Mom?"

"Yes?"

"I wish he wasn't getting married. I wish—"

"I know what you wish," she interrupted him. "You wish your real mother were still alive so the three of you could be a family."

But even if Melissa were alive, nothing would be different. Alex would still be marrying Isabella. Phillip's fantasy wasn't written in the stars.

She sat up. "Do you know what I think?"

"What?"

"We need to go home tomorrow and let him get married." I need to get as far away from him as possible. "After his honeymoon I'm sure he'll want you to come and stay with him until school starts."

"But you won't be here."

"No. My home is in Denver, but you have two homes now."

"I don't want two homes. Steve hates it."

"You never told me that before," she said and slid to the edge of the bed. "No matter what, you've finally been united with your father. Just remember that last week you didn't even know him or know where he lived."

"I know."

She could hear the tears in his voice.

"Do you like it here, Phillip?"

"I *love* it. Do you?"

If ever she heard a searching question, that was it. "Who wouldn't love Switzerland. It's out of this world."

"Dad's so fun. I don't want to leave, but I don't want you to go." Moisture bathed his cheeks. He burrowed his head in her shoulder.

"I have to go home, sweetheart."

He sniffed. "Then I guess I'll go with you. Isabella won't want me around for all their wedding stuff."

Such a gut-wrenching dilemma for a twelve-year-old. It thrilled her he loved Darrell that much, but her heart ached for him.

"Tell you what. I'm not feeling as nauseous as before. Let's spend the rest of today with your father."

"Honest?"

"Yes."

Because Phillip had made a decision, she could get through a few more hours in Alex's company knowing other people would be around.

"When he comes back with us to say good-night, then you can tell him we're flying home the minute we can make reservations."

"Okay."

"Think of all the fun stuff you have to tell your friends. You can show them the pictures you've taken. They'll love all the souvenirs you bought them the other day with the boys. Especially all that Swiss chocolate!"

"Yeah."

With the matter settled for the time being, they both freshened up before leaving the castle. Phillip knew the way to the pale yellow palace located on the west end of the grounds. It lay nestled amidst a grove of giant trees like a hidden jewel.

"Hey, Mom—don't you think this place looks like that house in *Sound of Music*?" They'd just entered the courtyard where water had pooled here and there because of the storm.

"A little, but this is much grander."

"Vito said their grandparents live here with them."

"How lucky the boys are to have Evelyn's parents around now that their father is gone."

"Not *her* parents, Mom. They live in Bavaria. I'm talking about dad's aunt and uncle, but they're away on a trip right now. Jules says his Grandpa Vittorio is mean."

"Is that description yours or his?"

"His. He says Vito's afraid of him."

That didn't sound good.

Phillip knocked on the door, breaking her train of thought. Soon a maid answered followed by the boys.

Once inside the elegant foyer flanked by various rooms,

Darrell marveled over the twin staircases on either side rising like a swan's neck to the second floor.

The beauty and symmetry of the architecture was stunning.

"I've always loved this palace." Alex's deep voice came from somewhere behind her.

She swung around and discovered him standing next to a very pretty brunette woman. She appeared to be in her early thirties.

"Evelyn and Darrell? It's time you two met."

"Hello," Darrell said first and extended her hand. "Thank you for inviting us to your home. I've been anxious to meet you. Your boys are charming."

Evelyn flashed her a friendly smile. "So is Phillip. I don't believe this family has ever had so much excitement."

"I'm sure you haven't," Darrell said.

Thankfully the other woman didn't sound judgmental, which was more than Darrell could have hoped for.

"Come in and sit down."

The room they entered was surprisingly comfortable and modern in its decor. Darrell found the nearest chair. Alex remained standing while Evelyn took a place on one of the couches opposite her.

"We're expecting Aunt Katerina any minute. I was so wishing you would recover enough to make it."

Alex's mother was coming, too? Darrell had hoped to avoid meeting her this trip, but maybe it was better to get it over with. After all, she was Phillip's grandmother.

"I'm feeling better, thank you. It will be an honor to meet her."

Evelyn cocked her head. "I can't believe Alex talked you into going down under the castle. Charles could never get me near it."

"I'm afraid Phillip wouldn't have let me live it down if I hadn't joined in."

"Jules was very impressed with you. It was the boys' first time ghost hunting. He told me I had to go next time."

Alex chuckled. "If you two will excuse me, I believe mother has arrived."

After he left the room Evelyn confided, "Another Valleder in the family has already transformed my boys' lives. What's amazing is how much they look alike. All three could be brothers."

Darrell nodded. "That's what I was thinking earlier. If I didn't know better, I would have thought they were all Alex's children."

"Vito reminds me of Alex's father, very serious and steady. Jules on the other hand has a happy-go-lucky temperament, more like my husband's."

Darrell's glance darted to a credenza against the wall. "Is that a picture of your husband?"

"Yes, that's Charles."

"I'm so sorry about his accident."

"So am I…" Her voice trailed.

"May I look at it?"

"Of course." She got up and handed it to Darrell. "It's a family portrait of the four of us taken a few months before his plane crashed."

"I don't know how you lived through it," Darrell murmured, fighting tears.

"I'm afraid I'll never get over losing him."

As Darrell studied it, she was astonished to discover that Alex's cousin looked enough like him to be his brother. In fact the more she looked at the picture, the more she noticed striking similarities between the boys' father and Phillip. If he was as wonderful as Alex, she couldn't imagine how Evelyn was functioning.

"Darrell?"

At the sound of Alex's voice she glanced over at the entry, almost dropping the picture.

"I'd like you to meet my mother, Katerina Valleder."

The lovely brown-haired woman possessed all the style and grace of a former queen. At a glance Darrell could see she'd bequeathed her good looks to her son who was devastatingly attractive in a formal, dark blue suit. The pristine white shirt and specially monogrammed tie with the Valleder crest proclaimed him the royal head of their centuries-old dynasty.

She got up from the chair. "How do you do, Mrs. Valleder." They both shook hands. Darrell knew that wasn't the way his mother was normally addressed. No doubt people said "Your Highness." Yet Alex had made it easy for Darrell.

He made everything easy. She trembled to realize she'd never be able to banish his image from her mind, or heart.

His mother's gray eyes studying Darrell so intently reminded her of the man who haunted her dreams. "It's a pleasure to meet the mother of my grandson."

"Thank you. He has yearned for a grandmother since he was old enough to ask why he didn't have one like his friends."

Alex took that moment to tell his mother what Phillip had said on the jet about the queen-size bed. The older woman actually laughed and Evelyn joined in. When it subsided she said, "I see you're holding a picture of Evelyn's family."

"Yes. We were just remarking on the dominance of the Valleder genes."

Katerina nodded. "After spending a few hours with the boys, I've decided Phillip is a composite of all the men in our family."

Emotion welled up in Darrell to realize her son came from a great heritage. Whatever their true feelings, these women *were* great to be kind and gracious to her and Phillip. Their impeccable breeding could be a model for others.

Melissa had gravitated to Alex, instinctively recognizing

without knowing that he was a man hewn from clay reserved for those with a special destiny.

"I wish you could have seen the boys' eyes once we started down that spooky staircase with Alex today. They're all so cute—"

"Aren't they?" Evelyn's eyes had grown moist.

Darrell handed the picture back to her. She set it on the table, then smiled.

"Now that everyone's here, shall we go in to dinner? It's ready."

Alex escorted his mother across the foyer to the charming dining room. Jules took over and helped her to her seat at one end of the table. Vito assisted his mother to the chair next to her.

Not to be outdone, Phillip—a quick study—came around and guided Darrell to her place opposite Evelyn. It was a first for him. Judging by the mirthful glance Alex flashed Darrell, he knew it, too.

Enjoying the moment too much, she averted her eyes while he sat down at the head of the candlelit table. It was resplendent with royal Valleder china and silverware placed on the cutwork lace linen.

He patted the chair on his right side for Phillip to join him. Once he was seated, Alex looked at his nephews. They weren't really his nephews, but as he'd told her and Phillip, he felt like their uncle. "Who wants to say grace?"

Darrell fought not to laugh at the dismay on their faces.

"Maybe Phillip would like to say it," his mother suggested.

"Sure, Grandma."

He folded his arms, closed his eyes and gave the usual prayer Darrell had taught him to say over the food.

After a collective "amen," Alex thanked him, then two of the staff began serving dinner.

Darrell was so proud of Phillip right then she could have burst. Though he was like an unpolished diamond and always would be, he had his shining moments and this had been one of them.

She saw the tender look Alex gave his son. It dissolved Darrell's bones.

No sooner had they started to eat than his cell phone rang. She noticed him glance at the caller ID, then get up from the table. "Excuse me for a moment."

The moment turned into twenty minutes. By the time he came back in the dining room, they were finishing their strudel dessert.

"I'm sorry, but something important has come up and I have to leave."

"Are you going to San Ravino to see Isabella?" Phillip asked the question no one else dared.

"Yes."

"When will you be back?"

"Tomorrow."

A crestfallen look crossed over Phillip's face, one everyone could see.

"Thank you for dinner, Evelyn."

"It was my pleasure."

Darrell knew everyone at the table was thinking how outspoken Phillip had been. It was something they would have to get used to because he'd been born with that trait. She couldn't look at Alex right then.

"I'll take Darrell and Phillip home when I go," Katerina spoke up.

"Thank you, Mother. I'll see you tomorrow, Phillip."

"Sure, Dad."

Alex flashed Darrell a hooded glance she couldn't decipher before he departed. It left her shaken. Did he kiss Isabella with the same passion he'd kissed her? Was he counting the minutes until they were together? Darrell couldn't take much more of this.

Ten minutes after he'd left the palace she heard the helicopter taking off. Phillip's expression mirrored her spirits, which had plummeted to a new low.

"Good afternoon, gentlemen."

Alex looked around the oval conference table in his office where his executive staff and ministers were assembled. Leo exchanged a private nod with him.

"I can only recall two times since I became king that I've had to call for an emergency session. Both times were due to the threat of a student uprising. This time the situation is different.

"I just flew back from San Ravino. After a great deal of soul searching over the past few days, Isabella and I have decided to call off our wedding."

The silence that filled the room was deafening.

"I've prepared a statement for the press, which I've given to Carl. Regardless of what you might hear, the princess and I parted on amicable terms."

More silence, the kind produced by shock reverberated throughout his office.

"As all of you have heard by now, very recently I discovered I have a twelve-year-old son who was born and raised in Colorado in the United States without my knowledge.

"The king could have ignored the revelation, but the man could not. Phillip Collier is my flesh and blood. I love him and have claimed him.

"Because of this action I'm fully aware that public sentiment will go against me. If I think it's for the good of the country, I'll step down."

At this point many heads had lowered, but not Leo's. The other man's eyes remained suspiciously bright.

"I recall a conversation I once had with father. He told me he didn't have any friends. His comment hurt me. When I asked him why, he said, 'That's the definition of a king.'

"I didn't understand what he meant, but I do now. No matter what decision you make as sovereign, you're going to hurt someone.

"By recognizing my son, I dare say I don't have a friend left, starting with the great men I've let down assembled in this historic conference room.

"But when I met Phillip for the first time and he said, 'You're my dad,' something went through me I can't describe. All I know is, I wanted to be all the things I could see in his eyes."

He cleared his throat. "Thank you for coming, gentlemen. That's everything."

On his way to his inner office to phone Darrell, Carl intercepted him. "Your Majesty? While you were in conference, Ms. Collier phoned to say that in case you were wondering, she and your son have gone into town to do some shopping for a few hours."

Disappointed they weren't immediately available, he thanked Carl before ringing Rudy. "How long ago did Ms. Collier leave the castle?"

"The car just pulled away."

"Alert the guard at the outer gate to prevent them from leaving the grounds."

Without conscious thought Alex left his office via a private staircase. Summoning his driver, he climbed in the back of his limo and told him to head for the north gate. He didn't expel a breath until he saw the limo between the security men's cars stopped at the gate.

Alex jumped out of the car before it had pulled to a stop.

* * *

"Hey, Mom? There's Dad!"

Darrell's hands clutched the armrests. What a fool she was to think she and Phillip could slip away from him, even for a few hours. At this point she was afraid to spend any more time with him.

When he suddenly climbed in the limo and sat across from her next to Phillip, the blood pounded in her ears.

His gaze narrowed on her face. "I got your message, but you can't go shopping yet or you'll spoil my surprise."

The car started to move, but instead of going to the castle, it appeared to be headed toward another part of the grounds.

Darrell's body trembled. She couldn't take another one of his surprises, let alone handle being in his presence a second longer.

"Will I like it?" Phillip teased.

"It's guaranteed."

"Where are we going?"

"You'll find out."

Eventually the limo pulled up to one end of the stable.

Phillip darted her an excited glance. Darrell had an idea Alex was going to give him his own horse. The boys each had a pony.

Alex turned to his son. "Go inside that door. It leads to the vet's office. He's waiting for you."

"The vet?"

"Yes. I'll be along in a minute."

On a new burst of energy, Phillip climbed out of the limo and sprinted inside.

"Alex—I'm glad we're alone because there's something important I have to tell you, and—"

"Isabella has called off the wedding," he broke in on her. "Permanently."

"Oh, no—"

The stabbing pain of guilt drove Darrell from the car. She headed blindly for the castle, running faster than she'd ever run in her life. But she couldn't outrun the limo. It drove alongside her until she slowed down and Alex urged her to climb back in.

Embarrassed to have caused a scene, she did his bidding. He didn't say anything until they'd arrived at the castle and he'd escorted her to the apartment she and Phillip had barely vacated. Once he'd opened the door for her, he followed her inside.

She whirled around, wet-faced. "Let me talk to Isabella in person. I can fix this."

He shook his handsome head. "This can't be fixed."

"Of course it can! She's in pain and frightened. Any woman would be. I don't care if she was raised a princess. She's never been married, and she wants it to work! I need to reassure her she has nothing to fear from Phillip."

He studied her through veiled eyes. "It's not Phillip she's worried about."

"Then what?" She kept wiping her eyes.

"I'm afraid it is I she doesn't trust."

"Of course she does. Otherwise she would have broken her betrothal to you long ago. Please let me try to appeal to her. I'll be happy to fly there right now if she wants."

"That would be like pouring acid on an open wound."

"Why?" she cried out aghast.

He rubbed the back of his neck. "You really need me to spell it out?"

"Yes!"

His gaze played over her features. "She says I'm different since coming back from Denver. She senses something she's never felt before."

"That's because you just found out you're a father. Of course you're different. Your entire world has been turned upside down."

"True, but this is something apart from Phillip."

She feared what was coming but she faced him without averting her eyes. "What exactly?"

"Contrary to what you overheard the desk clerk tell that tourist the day you were checking out of the Hotel Otter, Isabella and I were never a love match. But both of us were willing to fulfill our royal duty in the hope that love would grow."

She swallowed hard. "Didn't you ever sleep together?"

"No."

"Because of rules?"

"No."

"Didn't she ever want to?"

"Yes."

Darrell reeled from his blunt honesty. His admission brought her indescribable joy, but she could never let him know that.

"When I told her I had a son, it changed how Isabella feels about me."

"But that was thirteen years ago when you were only what? Twenty? Did you tell her Melissa died so she doesn't need to feel threatened?"

He didn't answer right away.

Her eyes widened. "She still thinks *I'm* that woman doesn't she!" Darrell's body started to shake. "How could you do that to her? To me?" She thumped her chest.

"I need to tell you a story first."

"I don't want to hear it!" she raged while he stood there as calm as a summer morning.

"You'll want to hear this one. The whole good of the monarchy hangs in the balance."

Put like that in such a solemn tone, he'd left her little choice but to listen.

"Let's go out to the balcony."

She didn't want to go anywhere with him, but he left her alone in the drawing room, expecting her to come to him. She could either comply with his wishes or string this out until she had a heart attack.

Defeated, she chose the former and found him staring out over the placid water that had formed whitecaps in yesterday's storm.

He must have sensed her presence. "I wish you could have met my cousin, Chaz. It's the name I made up for him because he didn't like the name Charles."

Darrell blinked in surprise.

"We were the same age. He could be a hellion. That's what made him so fascinating to me. Growing up I suppose you could say he was my alter ego.

"When I was old enough to read, my father put a little sign at the top of my bathroom mirror. It said, "One day you'll be king. Remember.""

A moan escaped her throat.

He turned to her. "I agree it was a terrible thing to do to a child. Uncle Vittorio was no different. If anything happened to father or me, the line of succession would go to him and eventually Chaz.

"At times he could be cruel, even abusive. He was a man who believed in corporal punishment to curb any rebellion in his son. When Chaz started drinking too much, I understood. He came to me when things got bad with my uncle. I often covered for him. That's why he gave me that ring."

Darrell's stomach lurched remembering what Phillip had said about the boys' grandfather being mean. How awful they had to live in such close proximity to him.

"My uncle was very ambitious, and still is. He would do most anything to be king, and has resented the fact that Chaz died instead of me."

"That's horrible," she whispered.

"In order to honor my promise to Father to marry Isabella,

I'd hoped she could get past this and agree to go ahead with the wedding while believing you are his birth mother."

"I still don't understand why you haven't told her the truth."

He eyed her balefully. "Because up to now it's been less complicated this way. The truth wouldn't change the fact that I fathered a son with a woman from my past. That's what has hurt Isabella.

"However once my uncle learns of Phillip's existence and discovers you didn't give birth to him, he'll enjoy humiliating you and the memory of your sister. It could bring up a lot of unnecessary pain which could end up hurting Phillip. As it is, I fully expect my uncle to rally the cabinet to repudiate me and my bastard son, forcing me to step down so he can be king."

The air got trapped in her lungs. "Your own uncle would do that?"

Lines of strain bracketed his mouth. His expression haunted her. He unexpectedly moved toward her and cupped her face in his hands. "The new millenium hasn't changed the nature of some men," his voice grated.

"Does your mother know the wedding is off?"

"Yes."

"Does she know about Melissa?"

"Yes."

"I'm glad you told her the truth, but she must be devastated!"

"I'm not going to pretend she's happy about my broken engagement, but one look at Phillip caused her to accept him as her grandson. That in itself is an indication of where her true heart lies."

She bit her lip. "There's absolutely no chance of Isabella changing her mind?"

"None. If there were no Phillip, we would have gone through with the wedding and done our best to make a good life together. But Phillip's existence has changed destiny. Now Isabella will have a chance to find the kind of love she's seen with some of her friends' marriages."

Darrell's eyes played over his face. "And what about you?"

"Does it matter? After what I've told you, you have every right to loathe me. As my father once told me, a king has no friends because every decision he makes offends someone."

Darrell didn't want to hear about all the damage his father and uncle had done to him. "Let's leave my feelings out of it," she blurted. "What's going to happen when the country hears you're not getting married?"

"I guess I'm going to find out. It'll be on the five o'clock evening news."

"Already?" The thought of Alex being forced to abdicate tortured her.

"I've just come from a cabinet meeting where I explained the situation and gave a statement to the press. If there's a groundswell of resentment against me, I'll step down."

"What exactly did you tell them?"

When she heard everything she felt ill.

"This is all because of *me*." She buried her face in her hands. "My trip to Bris has ruined your life."

"It gained me a son, Darrell," his voice shook. "No man could receive greater news."

Her head flew back. "But you're no ordinary man—" The tears streamed down her cheeks. "You're a king who might have to give up everything."

His eyes blazed with green fire. "*You* gave up everything for Phillip. Do you regret it?"

"Of course not!" she cried.

"Then we understand each other," he said on a note of finality.

While she stood there shivering, his cell phone rang. He answered it and spoke in Romanche for a few minutes. When he clicked off he said, "Something's come up. I have to get back to my office. Tell Phillip I'll phone him as soon as I'm free."

She watched his hard-muscled body leave her bedroom. The second she heard the outer door close, she flung herself on the bed and sobbed. Fifteen minutes later she was still agonizing over the reason for his broken engagement when she heard her animated son calling to her.

Jerked back to the present, she rolled off the bed and stood up, smoothing the hair out of her eyes. "I'm in my room, sweetheart. What is it?"

"You won't believe it. Dad got me a dog! It's a St. Bernard from that monastery in the Alps I told him I saw on television. It's the kind I always wanted. He's beautiful."

As her son came running into the bedroom, he was crying for happiness. A St. Bernard was his dream dog, but the condo didn't allow pets, not even miniatures.

"I'm going to train him how to save me and bring me drinks in a keg."

Darrell was in too much emotional turmoil to respond.

"He's almost all white and he's an older puppy because the monks weren't going to sell him, but they did it for Dad. I told him we wouldn't be back until after the wedding, so he's going to take care of him. But I wish we never had to go… Can I keep him, Mom?"

He wanted her permission.

"Mom?" he asked tentatively. "You've been crying, huh. Did you tell Dad to send the dog back? Is that why you didn't come inside the vet's office?"

"No, sweetheart. Of course you can keep him."

"Then what's wrong? Did you two have a fight? Where is he?"

"He's in his office working."

After calling off a royal wedding the entire country had

been looking forward to, he was probably trying to put out a dozen fires at once.

"Can I phone him?"

"After the great amount of trouble your father has gone to, I know he'd appreciate a call from his son thanking him for the dog."

"I love you, Mom." Almost knocking the wind out of her with his hug, he reached for the phone.

CHAPTER EIGHT

"YOUR MAJESTY? Your son is on line two."

"Thank you, Carl." He shoved his paperwork aside and turned on the speaker. "Phillip?"

"Dad—Thanks for the dog. I love him more than anything! Mom says I can keep him. You're the best! I love you."

Alex realized that Darrell was going to leave it up to him to tell Phillip about the wedding being called off. Nothing could have pleased him more.

He got up from the chair. "I love you, too, and I think this calls for a celebration. Why don't you and your mother come to my apartment in an hour and we'll have an early dinner together."

"I can't wait!"

The lump was still lodged in his throat. "Neither can I. See you soon."

The second Phillip hung up, Alex called the kitchen to arrange for dinner to be sent up, then he left the office for his suite.

He showered and dressed in a sport shirt and slacks, unable to remember the last time he'd been this excited about anything.

Heaven forgive him but he hadn't given Isabella a thought since he'd kissed her a final goodbye.

If ever he needed proof that a marriage between them

would have been dead wrong, the euphoria he was feeling right now was it.

He'd instructed his staff to set the table on the terrace off the sunroom. It overlooked the ancient part of the city with its cobblestoned streets and Romanesque churches. Phillip would enjoy looking through the binoculars.

As he went to the bedroom to get them, his cell phone rang. He checked the caller ID and clicked on.

"Mother?"

"Whatever you're doing, I have to talk to you now."

He gripped the phone tighter. "What is it?"

"I just had a phone call from Carl. Your uncle heard the news through a palace source. He and Renate have cut short their trip. They're on their way home."

Alex wasn't surprised. "If he thinks he can put me and Isabella back together again, I have news for him."

"That's not his agenda, Alex. It never has been," his mother confessed.

His brows knit together. "What are you talking about?"

"When your cousin died, and you still didn't seem eager to marry Isabella, it was Vittorio's intention to talk you into marrying Evelyn."

Evelyn?

Alex was dumbstruck.

"Finding out you and Isabella are not getting married is the reason he'll be arriving before morning. Carl let me know Vittorio has been secretly calling cabinet members to form a coalition forcing you to marry Evelyn for the good of the monarchy. He expects you to send Darrell and your son packing."

Over the years Alex had tried to control his anger against his uncle for the way he'd treated Chaz. But by trying to pull off a coup like this to get closer to the crown, he'd started a war. One Alex vowed his uncle wouldn't win.

"He's out of his mind. It'll never happen."

"I'm afraid his jealousy of your father has driven him beyond rationality."

"Dad?" a voice called out. "We're here!"

"Mother? I'm sorry but I have to go. Thank you for telling me this. I'll be in touch later." He clicked off.

"Come out on the terrace."

In a few seconds his son ran in to thank him again. Alex leveled his gaze on Darrell.

The white sundress against her golden skin was as stunning as her hair. The last rays of sun picked out the individual strands of gold and silver. Combined with eyes of amethyst, he couldn't look anywhere else.

"I'm going to call him Brutus."

With that declaration Alex was forced to pay attention to his son.

"It's the perfect Roman name."

"This is a fantastic view of the city," Darrell murmured. "It's like being in the helicopter."

"Try these." As Alex handed her the binoculars he'd brought out, her flowery fragrance swept him away.

He noticed her hands weren't quite steady as she lifted them to her eyes.

"How incredible. You have to see this, Phillip." Ignoring Alex, she handed him the glasses.

"Whoa—You can see everything!"

"From the time I was old enough to wander around by myself I always loved this view. So did Chaz. He would bring over his telescope and we would spy on people. When my father caught us, we were permanently banned from this apartment."

Phillip laughed. "I bet you got in a lot of trouble."

Darrell didn't want to think about what form it had taken for Chaz.

"Hey, Dad, what's the secret about the apartment Mom and I are staying in? Jules and Vito said nobody ever gets to stay in there."

Phillip wasn't the only one who was curious. Darrell had been dying to know.

"That's because down through the centuries it's been reserved as the bridal chamber after a royal wedding."

Darrell tamped down her moan.

"The rest of the time it remains vacant."

"You mean it's never been used since Aunt Evelyn and Uncle Charles got married?"

"That's right. At least not officially. Unofficially Chaz and I sneaked in there and slept in our bedrolls many times. We got a huge kick out of knowing that no one else in the castle knew what we were doing."

"That's so cool. If I could live anywhere in the castle, that's the place I'd choose."

"I figured as much, so I decided to let you stay in it."

"Are you and Isabella going to use it? You know, after you get married?"

A band constricted Darrell's lungs while she waited for Alex's answer.

"No."

"How come?"

He put an arm around Phillip's shoulders, guiding him to the table. "Because Isabella and I decided to call off the wedding."

Phillip's head jerked around. His face had closed up. "Because of me, huh."

"No."

"You don't have to lie, Dad. Isabella hates me. That's why she broke up with you."

"Hate's a strong word. I'm afraid she can't get over the fact that I met your mother first."

"You couldn't help that!"

"You're right. We agreed Isabella needs to be the first and only woman in her future husband's life."

"Do you feel awful?"

"I would if I didn't know that deep down she'll be a lot happier with someone else."

"Aren't you going to miss her?"

"Not in the way you mean. I wasn't in love with her. We didn't ever date the way your mom has done with Jack. It's not the same thing."

"Does this mean you have to find another princess to marry?"

"Actually I don't have to do anything."

When that news sank in, Phillip's smile returned. "That's because you're the king."

Alex's mouth curved into an irresistible smile. "For once that makes me really happy." He looked at Darrell with an almost triumphant gleam as he said it. She glanced away for self-preservation and found a place at the table.

They all sat down to eat.

"Hey, Mom—we don't have to go home now. Can Brutus sleep in my room? I promise to do all the work."

Darrell had just unfolded her napkin. "Why don't we talk about that later."

"I think now is a good time," Alex inserted. "Whenever I have a problem to solve, I call my cabinet together and each one of them presents their point of view. Why don't you go first? Tell your mother and me what you think would be best for your happiness."

Phillip put down his empty milk glass and stared soberly at his father. The white moustache added to the poignancy of the moment. "I wish Mom and I could live here with you all the time."

Alex nodded. "That idea makes me the happiest, too. What about you, Darrell?"

He hadn't helped the situation with that kind of input. Her emotions were too churned up to think or eat.

"I have a life and a job in Denver, but you can stay with your father for the rest of the summer. We'll e-mail each other every day. It'll work."

"You could get another job here."

"I'm sure I could, but our situation isn't like anyone else's. Your father is a world figure who leads a public life, so he has to live above reproach."

"What does that mean?"

She sucked in her breath. "It means no one would respect him if his son's mother were to live here, too. People can be cruel about things they don't understand. A king who doesn't have the respect of his people is no king at all.

"When I say I can't live here I mean not in this castle, this town or this country. It would never look right."

Phillip fought tears. An uncomfortable silence ensued. Finally he said, "I don't feel like eating."

Darrell could relate.

"Can I go say good-night to Brutus?"

"All right, but don't be too long."

He stood up eyeing them both. "I wish…oh forget it," he muttered and ran out of the apartment.

"If you can't guess what he wanted to say, I can," Alex drawled.

By now Darrell was a trembling mass of feelings. "This is an absurd conversation. Phillip knows you have to marry royalty."

"You're wrong. I told him I didn't have to do anything because it's true. I can conduct my personal life as I wish. If I want to marry you, I can," he added.

"How many of the kings before you have married a nonroyal?"

"None. They've gotten around it by having mistresses, but that's not my style. There's no law against a so-called mixed marriage, only against our children inheriting the throne."

Our children?

"How about it, Darrell? Would you like to take me on as your husband?"

She pasted a superficial smile on her face. "I've decided you have a lot more of Chaz in you than I originally thought."

"We weren't cousins for nothing. Since my first attempt to get married for the good of the monarchy has failed, and you've rejected Jack's proposal, why don't we enter into an arranged marriage for the noblest of reasons. *Our* son.

"For one thing it will solve the 'beyond reproach' problem.

"For another, my mother will be relieved I'm no longer a good for nothing bachelor. Best of all, our son will be elated."

Darrell jumped up from the table. "Don't say any more. This isn't a joke."

His gaze trapped hers. "I do know the difference. In this case I think Phillip's idea is brilliant even if he didn't come right out and say the words."

Suddenly Alex was on his feet, an imposing figure. "Darrell Collier? Will you marry me and come live at my castle with me and our son until death do us part and beyond?"

Her heart was thundering in her chest. "This is preposterous!" She was shaking so hard she had to hold on to the back of the chair. They faced each other across the table. As long as it was there between them, she felt a little more protected.

"Phillip confided that you don't like me very much because I hurt your sister. I can understand that. It's something I'm going to have to work on if you'll give me the chance."

Darrell moaned. That day in the mountains when they'd

kissed each other like two desperate lovers made a mockery of Phillip's remark.

"I know you don't hate me," he continued in that deep cadence. "At least not for what I did to your sister. So I'm assuming you've allowed Phillip to go on thinking something that isn't true for another reason altogether."

Her proud chin lifted. "Then please allow me to keep my reason to myself."

"Of course. But that doesn't have to stop us from getting married to give Phillip the family he's always yearned for. If the ceremony is performed soon, it will make the most sense.

"Everyone will realize ours was a real love match, the kind that produced a son long before we took our vows. Isabella will be vindicated in her feelings. It will help her to recover faster knowing I married for love."

Darrell wished he'd stop talking. She couldn't take any more.

"In view of our feelings for each other, people might tend to forgive me for unintentionally hurting Isabella. They understand a true romance when one comes along. A wedding between a royal and a commoner who already have a son could set the seal on the future of the country, bringing us into the twenty-first century."

"Or turn everyone against you—" Her voice trembled.

"In case things get worse, I'll step down."

She tried to swallow, but couldn't. "You don't mean that."

He folded his arms. "Try me and see. Chaz and I used to talk about it all the time. Confronted with a choice, which I didn't have before Phillip came into my life, I'd rather be his full-time father in Denver."

She shook her head, causing her hair to swish against her burning cheek. "What kind of a king are you?"

"Certainly not the one my father envisioned."

"You know what I meant, Alex. Don't patronize me over something this crucial."

"You think that's what I'm doing?" he fired back. "Your sense of duty makes you more fit to be a king's consort than any of the royal princesses I know.

"As I told you before, father would be proud of you. Maybe appealing to your noblest instinct is the way to win you around."

"It's not a case of winning me around. I couldn't marry you under *any* circumstances."

"If I moved to Denver, marriage wouldn't be necessary. I'll buy me a mountain cabin with horses above Colorado Springs. Phillip can travel between our two homes, just like Steve does."

She lowered her head. "There's no use talking to you."

"I'm sorry you feel that way. You're free to leave my apartment at any time. But before you go, I have one more thing to tell you."

Her heart was bumping like an off-balance washing machine.

"I don't want to hear it. Every time you say something like that, I realize I'm in a little deeper, making it impossible to extricate myself."

His satisfied smile twisted her insides. "Then I guess you have some real soul searching to do."

Her nails bit into the skin of her palms. "Your mother wouldn't let you step down."

"Aside from the fact that my decision is law, I cut the apron strings when I was Phillip's age. I follow my conscience." His gaze impaled her. "Just as you followed yours when you came to the castle requesting an audience with me. Contrary to common belief, it isn't only mothers who run into a burning building."

When she saw the determination in his eyes, she knew this was no game. He was in deadly earnest.

It shook her so violently she had trouble catching her breath.

"You can't abdicate. This is your life. There are too many people depending on you. You can't do it. I won't let you do it."

"Good. Then we'll say our vows tonight in the chapel."

She broke into frightened laughter because he always meant what he said. Her eyes searched his. "Why tonight?"

"That was the one thing I still had to tell you. The news about Isabella and me has reached my uncle's ears. My source tells me he's coming back from his trip and will be here before morning. He's the prince of Plessur, the second most powerful man in the country next to the king.

"As I told you, he's always wanted the crown for himself and wants to force me to marry Evelyn in order to get closer to it. If he gets enough members of my cabinet behind him, things could get ugly."

Darrell's hand had gone to her throat. "What's wrong with him?"

"He's totally irrational right now, but if I pull a checkmate strategy tonight, my marriage to you will be a fait accompli. To try to undo it might prove more embarrassing to him than to me."

Darrell was aghast. "This is like something out of a Machiavellian drama."

His eyes had formed slits. "Welcome to my world."

"You're not joking. That's what is so frightening about this."

"I would never lie to you, particularly about something this vital. If we've said our vows by the time he arrives, it will make his position much more difficult."

Another shiver attacked her body.

"The sooner I make an honest woman of you, the faster the nine-day wonder will be over. Depending on how many friends I have at the highest government level, everything should get back to normal."

A cry escaped her lips. "When it comes to you, there's no such thing as normal."

What he'd just told her had sent her into shock.

"I'm a normal man, Darrell. In case you were wondering, I want you in my bed."

His stark frankness knocked the foundations out from under her.

"I plan to be your husband in every sense of the word. Don't tell me you'll marry me if you can't be a wife to me. Being around Phillip makes me hungry for another child."

"What if I can't?" her voice squeaked.

"Have children, you mean?"

"No. I meant, what if I can't marry you?"

A remote expression crossed over his rugged features. "In that case I'll move to Colorado Springs and make a new life for myself."

"You could marry another princess!"

"For you to say that means I never knew the real you."

She tossed her head. "I'm not sure who the real me is anymore. I only know that you'd be giving up the great heritage you were born to. Who would rule if you didn't?"

"Depending on public sentiment, my mother would act as regent until Vito comes of age at eighteen."

She groaned because there was no satisfactory solution.

He moved closer. "Having met Phillip, I've discovered fatherhood is more important than anything else. In time I hope to find a woman who wants me as much as I want her. Someone Phillip will like."

There wasn't a woman in existence who wouldn't want him. She needed to get away from him to think. While they'd been talking it had grown dark.

"I—I'd better go check on him."

She started walking through the sunroom to the outer door of his suite. He stayed where he was.

"I'll be by in a half hour to hear your answer."

After she closed the door, he pulled out his cell phone and called his mother.

"This isn't the king calling. This is your son begging for your help. I need you to phone the archbishop and ask him to come to the castle immediately. He'll do it for you."

His mother gasped. "You're going to marry Darrell."

He swallowed hard. "If she'll have me."

Now came the waiting. He needed his mother on his side. One minute turned into two.

"I'll call him now and tell him to meet us in the chapel."

His eyes misted over. "I've always loved you, but in case you didn't know it, this is your finest hour."

"I love and believe in you, Alex."

"Then I'm a lucky man."

"I'll gather those people closest to you."

"Bless you."

He clicked off. After clearing his throat he phoned Leo. His friend picked up on the second ring.

"Alex?"

"Are you in the city?"

"Yes. What can I do for you?"

"I think I'm getting married in a little while."

Leo let out a low whistle.

"It's the only way to do my duty and keep my son with me."

"I have to tell you you're the most courageous man I've ever known."

"Insanity runs in the family, Leo, but I'll be damned if I'll let Uncle Vittorio have any say in things. Would you believe he wants me to marry Evelyn? Of course it's never going to happen, and you and I both know why."

Though they'd never discussed it, Alex knew how Leo felt about her. He had a hunch Evelyn was starting to take an uncommon interest in his chief security man. Alex intended to keep helping that relationship along, but he had to work out his own destiny first.

In a few minutes he'd brought Leo up-to-speed about what was going on.

"I want you to place extra guards at all entrances to the castle ASAP. No one except the archbishop is to be let in."

"Understood."

"Should Uncle Vittorio decide to pay me a nocturnal visit, check with me first before allowing him in. By that time I should be a married man. I'll send Darrell and Phillip to the cabin in the Upper Ungadine by helicopter. Since the slide it's impossible to get to it without one. We'll have our privacy there.

"Vittorio will assume I'm enjoying the privileges of the bridal chamber in the Saxony apartment. It wouldn't surprise me if he barges right in. If he does, I'll be waiting for him."

"That could be dangerous."

"It's been coming on for a lifetime." Alex's voice grated. "As soon as I hang up with you, I'll dictate a press release for Carl to give the paper in the morning."

"Getting the people on your side this quickly could work, Alex. Everyone in the conference room was deeply affected by what you said."

"First I have to convince Darrell."

"If she's fighting you, then she's even more courageous than you are. I think you've met your match."

Alex knew he had…

"I've only got a few more minutes on my side to make a miracle happen."

"I'll take care of everything."

"I know you will. I owe you, Leo." Alex knew exactly how to render payment.

"It's an honor to serve you, Alex. We'll stay in contact."

Alex hung up, then started unbuttoning his shirt as he strode toward the wardrobe in his bedroom.

He opened the door and pulled out his ceremonial outfit that had been cleaned and prepared for his wedding to Isabella.

His gut was telling him he needed to pull out all the stops if he had any hope of getting Darrell to go along with his plans.

CHAPTER NINE

THE Valleder Canton is reeling tonight with the news that King Alexandre Phillip and Princess Isabella of San Ravino, Italy, have called off their wedding permanently.

In a speech made before his cabinet earlier today, the king stated that after a period of deep soul searching, they decided to break their engagement. He insisted their parting was amicable, and hopes the public will give the princess her privacy at this sensitive time.

Those sources closest to the king blame the breakup on the beautiful blond American woman he became involved with thirteen years ago. They have a twelve-year-old son together named Phillip.

Last week his mother, Darrell Collier, from Denver, Colorado, was seen at the castle taking a tour. Since then Phillip has been seen in Bris in the company of Princess Evelyn and young Princes Vito and Jules.

Certain sources have revealed that the king has always been in love with his son's mother, which is why he waited so long before making final wedding arrangements.

We have yet to hear from Princess Isabella's spokesperson, but there is speculation that public sentiment is building against the king who up until now has enjoyed unprecedented support, even subduing those protesters who want the monarchy abolished.

The news that he's been privately carrying on a torrid liaison with a commoner might just bring about an end to his six-year reign. There's speculation that Prince Vittorio of Plessur could ascend the throne but he hasn't been available for comment, nor has the Queen Mother, Katerina. This news has already impacted the stock market and several sensitive trade negotiations wi—

Unable to stand listening to anymore, Darrell shut off the TV and flew out to the balcony. Sick to her very soul, she stared down at the dark swirling water below.

Night lent a brooding element to the castle. In former times Alex's ancestors had counted on their forbidding fortress to intimidate their enemies from without its thick walls. Today Alex faced an enemy from within. But it had all started because she'd come looking for her son's father.

By finding Alex, she'd set off a chain of events that had put the monarchy in jeopardy just as she'd feared.

She couldn't undo the damage now, but she and Phillip could fly back to Denver and stay indoors. If they were out of reach of the press for a time, Alex could concentrate on what he had to do to secure his position without worrying about them.

His question was still ringing in her ears. *How about it, Darrell? Would you like to take me on as your husband?*

Surely he hadn't really meant it. It couldn't possibly work no matter how much he wanted Phillip with him. She had to get out of there.

"Mom?"

Her son came running in the apartment. "You should see Brutus. He's the cutest dog ever!"

Darrell left the balcony and hurried into the bedroom to

meet him. "I'm glad you're back, sweetheart, because we're leaving for Denver as soon as we can get packed."

On cue his face crumpled. "How come?"

"I'll tell you about it once we're on the royal jet."

"But I don't want to leave Dad."

"We have to." She grabbed her suitcase and started throwing things inside. "It's all over the news that the monarchy is in trouble. Every minute you and I are here, it causes more trouble for him. Please do as I say and get your things together."

"But, Mom—"

She rushed past him to find his suitcase and start gathering up his belongings. It didn't take her long. He followed her around in a daze.

When she'd finished, she phoned Rudy and told him to have the helicopter waiting out on the pad.

"Come on, Phillip. It's time to go." Carrying both cases, she started for the drawing room.

"Not so fast. I need an answer to my proposal first."

In the next instant Alex appeared in the doorway blocking her exit. His dark blond male virility dazzled her as did all six foot three of him. Her hands let go of the suitcases, which fell to the floor.

He'd dressed in the same splendid white ceremonial clothes he'd worn at his coronation. The royal-blue band stretching from the gold epaulet on his right shoulder and across his chest to the other side of his waist proclaimed him the king.

Again she realized the Internet picture couldn't possibly capture his spectacular living presence as monarch of the realm.

For once Phillip was absolutely speechless.

Alex flashed his son a smile that brought a lump to her throat. "I've asked your mother to marry me so we can be a family, Phillip. The archbishop is waiting in the chapel downstairs to perform the ceremony. But I think I've scared her."

Phillip turned to her with wounded eyes. "You really hate Dad, don't you."

"No, sweetheart—" she cried out. "That's not why I wanted to leave."

"Your mother thinks she can put me and Isabella back together if she returns to Denver, but that isn't possible. Isabella doesn't want to marry a man who already has a son he loves. I don't blame her."

"Neither do I," Phillip murmured. He stared at Darrell for a long moment. "If you're afraid my real mom will hate you for marrying Dad, you don't need to be. All this time I bet she's been hoping *you'd* find him and marry him."

Oh, Phillip.

Tears trickled down Darrell's cheeks. "Excuse us for a minute, Alex." She ushered him into his bedroom and shut the door.

His face gleamed with moisture. "I wish you would marry him, but I know you don't love him."

"Sweetheart, we've barely known each other a week!"

"I loved him the night he came to the condo."

"Because you knew he was your father."

"Yeah. But he's so awesome I bet you'd learn to love him if you'd give him a chance. Grandma told me she and Grandpa didn't like each other very much when they first got married. Then he got bucked off his horse because he wasn't a good rider. He got a broken leg so she had to take care of him. She said that's when they fell in love."

Darrell could hardly believe Katerina had confided that to Phillip.

"I can't see that happening to your father," she quipped to hide her tumult.

"Neither can I, but you know what I mean."

"I know what you mean."

"I love him so much. He's the best father in the whole world."

"Better than Ryan's dad?"

"Dad's not like anybody else. He's—"

"A super hero?" she found the words for him.

Phillip's moist eyes blazed with light. "Better! He's like somebody too good to be true, but he isn't. I mean he's alive and he's real and—"

"And you love him with all your heart."

"Yeah." He wiped his eyes.

She sucked in her breath. "If we become a family, it's possible Alex will have to step down from the throne."

"Why?"

Darrell explained what she'd seen on the TV. "That's why I wanted us to leave, to give Alex a chance to fight for his right to remain king without worrying about us."

"But he doesn't want us to go."

Her son spoke the truth. Becoming a father had transformed Alex. Though he'd proved to be the dutiful son, she realized there was a part of him that had longed to be a free spirit like his cousin.

She remembered what Alex's own father had put on his bathroom mirror. Darrell shuddered at the thought of being raised by such a stern, autocratic parent.

Her chest heaving, she looked all around. To agree to marry Alex meant all this would be her home from now on. It was a world so foreign to her, she still couldn't comprehend it.

If she said no to his proposal, he would still embrace fatherhood. He loved Phillip enough to give up the kingdom. But he would leave a heartbroken mother and family behind, not to mention a whole country who needed his unique strength and leadership.

If she said yes, it meant staying to fight for what was rightfully his. Knowing the history between Chaz and his father, she couldn't doubt Alex's conviction that his uncle was a frightening adversary.

Would it really come to a coup?

No one had the answers yet.

Only a few weeks ago she'd consulted a heraldry expert. If he'd told her that the king of Valleder would ask her to marry him within the month, she'd have laughed hysterically all the way home.

Jack had wanted to marry her. When she'd turned him down, she'd believed it was because Phillip manipulated him too easily. But that was just an excuse to put him off. The truth was, Jack had never set her on fire.

Only one man had ever managed to do that. Those thrilling moments in Alex's arms had taught her the true meaning of passion. She realized she could never marry a man unless he could affect her in the same way.

While they'd been fused together by the most overwhelming chemistry, she'd lost all awareness of her surroundings.

Alex said he wanted another child.

He'd said he wanted it with *her.*

Trembling with trepidation and excitement, she looked at Phillip. Her son eyed her with an earnestness and pleading that was her undoing. Taking a sharp breath she said, "Do you want to tell your father I'll marry him?"

Phillip gave a resounding whoop before running through to the other room. When Darrell caught up to him, he was already in his father's arms. The bear hug they gave each other was all the more touching because of his elegant attire.

"Phillip?" she reminded him from a short distance off, attempting to tamp down her secret joy. "You'd better hurry and get into the same outfit you wore to dinner with Isabella."

"I'll help you," Alex murmured. They went back in his bedroom. Within two minutes he was dressed. He lifted his head. "Dad? Since Mom has decided to marry you, you don't need to worry she hates you anymore."

As Alex performed his fatherly duty tying his tie, his eyes sought hers. She couldn't read their enigmatic expression. "This is it then." His voice sounded thick with emotion.

She didn't know if her heart could withstand the knowledge that she was about to become his wife.

"Yes. I-if you two will excuse me, I'll change."

Alex shook his head. "You're perfect as you are." His eyes made a slow sweep of her face and body. Warmth spread through her system, reminding her that he wanted a wife in the Biblical sense. "In that white dress you look like a royal bride. I thought as much when you came to dinner earlier."

The simple cap sleeves and full skirt were hardly the attire for the bride of a king, but there was no help for it now.

He patted Phillip's shoulders. "Shall we go?"

"I've never been to a wedding," Phillip said as they filed out of the apartment. "Do I have to do anything?"

"You're my best man so you'll stand on my other side while your mother and I exchange vows."

"That's all?"

"No. There's one more thing."

"What is it?"

Alex paused midstride. "When the archbishop tells me to give your mother the ring, you'll hand this to me." Alex reached in the right pocket of his trousers and pulled out a jeweled ring.

Phillip examined it. "Hey, Mom—this is heavier than the ring Dad gave me. It could weigh you down."

Alex chuckled. "Better put it in your blazer pocket until time. It's seven hundred years old."

"Seven hundred?"

From a long distance off Darrell could see Alex's mother standing at the doors of the chapel in a ceremonial white dress and tiara.

When she smiled, Darrell wanted to cry because it looked so sincere.

Out of love for her son and the good of the monarchy she was willing to help carry off this charade. Whatever her true feelings, her behavior would lead anyone to think she was happy about this unorthodox alliance so soon after Alex's broken engagement.

In a surprise move she draped a white lace mantilla over Darrell's hair. It fell to her waist. Borrowed or new, it made Darrell feel bridal and more prepared to enter the church.

His mother kissed her forehead, then Phillip's cheek. Lastly she kissed her son on both cheeks before walking inside. The three of them followed her into the large, dimly lit interior. But for the frescoes, the medieval atmosphere gave Darrell the impression she'd been sent back in time.

"Are you sure there's only one ghost haunting this castle?" she whispered unsteadily.

Alex slid his hand beneath her veil and rested it on her waist to guide her up the center aisle. "Stay close to me. I won't let any harm come to you."

His touch sent little shivers of delight through her nervous system.

Sixty or so men and women obviously loyal to Alex had assembled, but her attention was focused on the archbishop in colorful vestments. He was a wiry man who stood waiting before the ornate shrine.

At their approach, he made the sign of the cross in front of Alex. "Your Majesty."

"Thank you for coming at this late hour, Your Grace," Alex said in English.

"Please meet my son, Phillip, and his mother, Darrell Collier."

The seventyish-looking man gave a slight nod to the two of them, but his eyes settled on Darrell.

"In entering into this union, you have a responsibility like no other. I will pray to God you are equal to it."

Darrell's mouth had gone dry. "Thank you, Your Grace. God has already been plagued by my prayers."

He studied her for another minute, pondering the veracity of her words. Suddenly he nodded as if in satisfaction.

Alex's hand gave her waist a reassuring squeeze.

The archbishop told Phillip to stand on the other side of his father. Afterward he summoned Alex's mother to stand next to Darrell.

"Let us pray."

Darrell bowed her head. From that point on they were treated to a ceremony in Romanche. She understood none of it, but it didn't matter and knew it didn't bother Phillip. When the ceremony was over, his parents would be married.

"Darrell Collier?" the archbishop unexpectedly said in English again. "Do you pledge your life and devotion to God and your liege unto death and beyond?"

"Yes," she said in a quiet voice.

"Alexandre? Do you pledge your life and devotion to God, country and your chosen bride unto death and beyond?"

"Yes," he proclaimed in a deep voice that reverberated in the vaulted interior.

"Take your bride's hand and bestow the ring."

Darrell felt him turn to Phillip before reaching for her hand. He slid the ring on her finger.

"You are now husband and wife in the sight of God. May He bless your union. May He guard you against all evil. In the name of the Father, the Son and the Holy Ghost, Amen."

"Amen," the congregation repeated.

"God save the king," the archbishop declared in a strong voice.

"God save the king," everyone said more forcefully.

Darrell didn't know the protocol at the wedding of a king, but evidently it wasn't that different when it came to the traditional kiss.

Alex pulled her close. "I've been waiting for this since that day on the mountain," he whispered.

She only had a brief glimpse of lambent hazel eyes before he covered her mouth in a kiss that let everyone know they'd done this before, that this was no arranged marriage.

But with an audience watching them, she couldn't respond with the same abandon as before.

What Alex didn't know was that the knowledge that she'd be alone with her new husband in a little while had caused a secret fire to burn hotter and brighter inside her.

Aware that everyone's attention was on them, she eased away as best she could, only to be confronted by the archbishop whose raisin dark eyes were smiling at her.

They wouldn't do that if he didn't approve of their marriage a little bit, would they? After all, he was supposed to have performed Alex's marriage to Isabella in the city's main cathedral.

"Welcome to our family, my dear," Alex's mother spoke behind her.

She swung around. "Thank you, Your Highness."

"Call me Katerina."

Her eyes stung. "I'd love to."

She grasped Darrell's hands. "You've transformed my son. I've never seen him like this before."

"Phillip has been transformed, too."

The older woman kept staring at her. "Whatever force is in play, I want you to know I'm on your side."

"You'll never know how much that means to me."

"When Alex is ready to share you, come and see me."

"I promise." Without conscious thought she hugged Alex's mother and received a hug back.

"Mom?"

Darrell let go of Katerina and turned to her son. He was grinning. In a quiet voice he said, "I guess you like Dad more than you thought, huh."

"I guess I do."

"Darrell?" Alex called to her. "I'm afraid we're in a hurry, but everyone wants to meet you before we leave. We have some papers to sign as well."

"Of course. I'm coming."

He put a familiar hand at the back of her waist and ushered her through to the anteroom off the chapel where she put her signature next to Alex's on their royal wedding certificate. When they'd finished business, Evelyn and the boys were first in line to congratulate them.

"It was the most touching ceremony I've ever seen. I wish my husband had been here to see how happy you've made Alex. I'm so glad he married you instead of Isabella," she said sotto voce.

There was a sweetness in Evelyn. Her words seemed to have come straight from her heart. It was another sign that Darrell had done the right thing.

"Thank you, Evelyn. I'm so glad to have a friend. Phillip loves you already."

Evelyn smiled through the tears. "Our boys are going to be inseparable from here on out."

"I know."

Darrell reached down to touch their cheeks.

Jules stared up at her. "Can we call you Aunt Darrell?"

"I want you to!"

"Darrell?" Alex grasped her hand. "I'd like you to meet my minister of communications."

For the next while she accepted the warm congratulations from people who were clearly behind Alex and wished them both well. It provided her a small glimpse into his world and what he would expect of her. No bride had ever married royalty more unprepared.

To her relief he finally told her they were leaving. He drew her through a door that led down a private passageway.

"Where's Phillip?"

"Mother's taken charge of him. He'll meet us at the helicopter."

They weren't spending the night in the Saxony apartment?

He'd opened it up for her and Phillip to stay there, yet it seemed he had no intention of honoring tradition by spending his wedding night there. Probably because she was a commoner. But somehow it hurt.

"Where are we going?" she asked, hoping her voice sounded level.

"It's a surprise. You and Phillip will fly there first. I'll follow."

A honeymoon à trois.

Why would she expect anything else? Alex enjoyed kissing her enough to marry her in order to keep Phillip an integral part of his life and hopefully have a child of his own.

But he wasn't in love with her!

One day the passion on his part would fade. If she kept that truth uppermost in her mind, their arranged marriage could work. As long as he never knew her deepest feelings.

When they came to another door he moved her against the wall. Keeping her there with his body, he lifted her chin with his hand. "Don't be alarmed if I don't join you until morning."

She started to panic. "Are you in danger?"

His brows furrowed. "Not in the way you mean. Leo, my head of security, just informed me Uncle Vittorio will be arriving by car in the next hour. I need to be here, but I don't want you or our son anywhere around. This king intends to honor his vow to be your devoted servant."

She knew his devotion would never be in question because that was the way he was made.

He lowered his head and pressed a long, hard kiss to her mouth. To convince her or himself?

When he raised up, she held herself rigid so he wouldn't notice how out of breath she was.

Without saying anything he opened the door that led to the outside of the castle. A limousine was waiting.

He helped her into the back seat. "Stay safe for me."

Another brush of his lips against hers and the car sped off in the darkness toward the helipad.

She pulled the mantilla off her hair so she could see out of the window better, but he'd disappeared. It wasn't until that moment she realized if anything happened to him—anything at all—she wouldn't be able to bear it.

Her heart gave a great lurch. Impossible as it might be after only one week, she knew she was painfully in love with him.

As her hand gripped the lace material, she became aware of the ring he'd given her. It was old, encrusted with jewels and too big for her.

She would need to examine the family heirloom in the light before she gave it back to him to keep with the crown jewels. This was a ceremonial ring only meant to be worn on an occasion like this.

Darrell was a Valleder now. She couldn't help but wonder what would have happened if she'd been the one working at that dude ranch rather than Melissa. Would he have fallen for Darrell because he couldn't help himself?

Could she have won Alex on her own power? Enough that he would have broken his betrothal to Isabella in order to marry Darrell?

Those were questions for which she had no answers.

To be loved for yourself and no other reason would bring the greatest happiness.

To Darrell's sorrow, she would never know that kind of joy because for one thing, Alex had married her to keep Phillip with him. For another, it was Isabella who'd broken the engagement, not the other way around. Those were two facts Darrell would always have to live with.

Maybe it was possible Alex would come to love her as Phillip had suggested, but she was selfish enough to wish he'd loved her at first sight.

Since Darrell had never believed in fairy tales like Melissa, why couldn't she be happy over what reality had presented her?

All of a sudden the door to the limousine opened, surprising her. "Where's Dad?"

"Hi, sweetheart. He had a few things to do and will join us in a little while."

"Where are we going?"

"He didn't tell me, but since it's your father we're talking about, I'm sure we'll love it."

"I wish he was here," he grumbled as they climbed into the helicopter. She echoed his feelings.

The pilot flashed them a broad smile. "Congratulations on your marriage, Your Highness."

"Thank you, but you don't need to call me that. I'm no royal princess. Darrell and Phillip will do just fine."

"Darrell it is. Alex has asked me to give you a moonlight tour of the Ungadine Valley on our way, so strap yourselves in."

"Cool!"

Once the rotors were whirring, they rose from the ground so fast

Darrell almost lost her stomach.

She looked below at the receding castle, experiencing a deep ache in her heart. Alex was down there waiting to face his uncle.

"Look, Mom. That's the ridge where we went horseback riding."

Phillip's enthusiasm would have to make up for both of them.

The Swiss Alps were one of the most beautiful sights on earth, yet she wouldn't be able to enjoy anything until she saw Alex again and knew all was well.

"Hey—what happened over there?" he asked the pilot.

"There was a forest fire followed by a rainstorm. It caused a huge mud slide."

"Was anybody hurt?"

"Fortunately not. This region is off limits to the public."

"How come?"

"Because this is your father's favorite mountain retreat."

"Where?"

"We're coming up on it in a minute. One of his staff is already there with your bags and will see to your needs."

Another pain stabbed Darrell. So this was what it was like to go on a royal honeymoon. No privacy from the retinue of people ready to serve their king.

Before long the helicopter set down in a clearing next to a tiny log cabin that looked like it had been there for years. A male staff member came out the door to greet them and show them inside.

The clean interior was sparsely furnished, providing just the basics. A log wall with a fireplace separated one little bedroom and bathroom from the kitchen cum living room area. Upstairs was a loft reached by split log steps. Phillip whooped with excitement, declaring that's where he would sleep.

After a meal of ham and cheese rolls served with salad and fruit, Phillip was ready to crash and went up to bed. Darrell changed into jeans and a T-shirt, then went upstairs with Phillip to wait for Alex.

Before going to bed, she opened the window to let in the night air. The temperature at the top of the world was much cooler than in the valley. But nothing could bring down the fever brought on by a longing to know her new husband's possession, even if only one of them was in love.

When she started to chill, she climbed under the covers next to Phillip and waited.

One hour turned into another. The night was endless. If she slept, she couldn't remember. It wasn't until morning she heard the long awaited sound of the helicopter. Was it getting ready to take off, or had it just landed?

She rolled over and sat up. Maybe Alex was here!

Phillip was still asleep. With her heart thudding, she threw off the covers to get out of bed and slammed into a powerful male body just entering the loft. Alex's arms went around her to steady her like they'd done on the jet.

He'd changed out of his royal attire and was wearing a burgundy polo shirt and khakis. But when she looked up at his face she saw a different man from the one who'd told her to keep herself safe for him.

Lines of tension defined his arresting features. His eyes had gone dark and looked so haunted, she knew something dreadful had occurred.

By now Phillip was awake. "What's wrong, Dad?"

She put a hand on his arm. "Tell us."

A pulse throbbed at the side of his mouth. "My uncle has suffered a minor heart attack."

"Oh, Alex—I can't believe it came to this. How serious is it?"

"Provided there are no complications, he should recover just fine. They'll probably send him home from the hospital tomorrow, but I'm afraid we'll have to go back to Bris. Everyone's at the hospital."

"Of course."

"I'll be dressed in a sec, Dad."

Darrell nodded. "I'll go downstairs and pack up my things."

He gripped her upper arms in front of Phillip. "I'd hoped to spend a week up here. Just the three of us without another soul or worry to disturb us. We'll come back here in a couple of days."

"That'll be great, Dad. I always wished we had a cabin!" Phillip called over his shoulder before leaving the loft with his suitcase.

Alex drew in a fortifying breath. "Of all the outcomes, this wasn't the one I'd anticipated."

"Don't you think I know that? Alex— Since this is life threatening, maybe Phillip and I should fly back to Denver for a while. You know. Just to stay out of the way while he's recuperating."

The second the words left her lips his expression turned black. His hands slid to her wrists. He looked pointedly at her hands devoid of jewelry.

"My ring kept slipping, so I removed it and put it in my purse for safe keeping," she explained in a rush.

His grimace deepened.

"We took sacred vows last night. Perhaps you didn't understand how binding they are, but it's too late for regrets. You're not going anywhere. We're husband and wife now, and that's the way it's going to stay."

He set her aside and left the loft ahead of her.

"Alex—" she called down to him, anxious to explain, but he didn't pause. She didn't dare shout at him in front of Phillip and his staff. That was the problem with going on a honeymoon that included more than two people!

She hadn't meant to upset him. He'd taken it all wrong because he didn't understand how guilty she felt about everything. His uncle was in the hospital because of her.

If she'd never come to Bris…

But she couldn't keep harking back to that. She *had* come, and it *had* turned the Canton on its ear exactly the way he'd prophesied.

They were in this together now. Alex expected her to hold up her end of the bargain.

She could hear her grandmother talking about Melissa's pregnancy. "Don't go on about it, Darrell. Spilt milk can't be put back in the bottle. We've got no choice but to help her and love her. That's all there is to it."

How Darrell had loved her pragmatic grandmother who'd sacrificed her whole life for them. About now Darrell needed to call on her grandmother's wisdom and try to live up to her example.

Knowing Alex was anxious to leave, she hurried below. If they were returning to the castle she needed to wear something dressier than casual clothes. The maid who'd packed her bag had included a print skirt and blouse. They would have to do. Once at the apartment she would shower and change into a suit to wear to the hospital.

"I've never even met your uncle. Do you think he'll die?" Phillip asked Alex on their flight back to the castle.

"Not if he follows doctor's orders. He needs peace and quiet. How would you like it if the boys slept in the Saxony apartment with you for a couple of nights?"

"That would be the best! I'll tell them to bring their sleeping bags and we'll camp out on the balcony."

"Sounds like a plan. I'll suggest they bring the telescope. You'll be able to see all kinds of animal life on the slopes beyond the lake."

"Is that okay with you, Mom?"

"Your mother will be sleeping in my apartment from now on. I've already had her things moved."

What Alex had just said was perfectly logical, yet Darrell

could scarcely breathe because he'd sounded possessive just now. It sent a little thrill through her body.

"You can move in there, too, Phillip. I have an extra bedroom."

Her hand clutched her purse tighter. Of course he wanted Phillip close to them.

"Or, you and Brutus can have the Saxony apartment to yourself."

Phillip's eyes rounded while Darrell's head lowered to hide her surprise.

"You mean the whole thing?"

"If you want. It would be a shame to lock it up again until somebody else in the family gets married."

"Like Vito or Jules, huh."

"Or you."

"But I'm not a prince."

"You're my son. That's all that matters."

CHAPTER TEN

DARRELL had never loved Alex more than at this moment.

When they arrived at the castle she hurried up to his apartment while he and Phillip went to get the boys.

She hadn't been in the suite long when her cell phone rang again. Jack had been calling her, but this time it was Danice. She picked up and said hello.

"Darrell? I can't believe what I've heard on the news in the last twenty-four hours. First it was announced that the king of Valleder broke his engagement to Princess Isabella. Then it was announced he had a twelve-year-old son and married his former lover who just happened to be *you*.

"I know you met a guy when you flew to Switzerland on vacation last week. I also know he asked you and Phillip to spend the Fourth with him. But you didn't tell me he was the king! He's the hunkiest male I've ever seen in my life.

"Jack called me a few minutes ago. He's positive it's a mistake, or else there are two Darrell Colliers. He's been trying to reach you. I've never heard him so upset and I've worked for him for a lot of years. Is it true? Did you really marry him this fast?"

Darrell bit her lip. "Yes, but don't believe all the gossip you've heard."

"Of course not. The media lies about everything. I know you adopted your sister's baby. What's the real truth?"

Darrell gripped her phone tighter. Danice didn't know anything about Darrell's reasons for going to Switzerland in the first place. "One day I'll tell you everything. It's very complicated. Suffice it to say neither Alex nor the princess were in love."

"Obviously not, otherwise he wouldn't have been a goner the second he met you. However for *you* to do something so out of character means he must really be something."

Her eyes closed. "He is," she said in a tremulous voice. "Listen Danice—I can't talk now. Alex will be coming any minute. Would you do me a favor and tell Jack I'll call him tomorrow? I need to turn in my resignation. I'll call you right after."

"I can't wait to meet your lord and master in person."

"He isn't like that."

"You sound different. Happy. If anyone deserves it, you do."

"People don't deserve things."

"They do when they're as selfless as you've been. Does Phillip like him?"

Tears threatened. "He adores him."

"Then the king must really be amazing because it took Jack a good year before Phillip gave him the time of day."

"I know."

There was a reason for that. It was called being father and son.

"I can tell you can't wait to be with your husband. Do you call him Your Highness when you're alone?" she teased.

Darrell chuckled. "No,"

"All right. I guess I'll have to wait to hear all the exciting details. You'd better call me."

"I promise."

After they hung up, Darrell started to empty her suitcase.

She'd been in Alex's apartment before, but Phillip had led her out to the sunroom. She'd only glimpsed the other parts of the suite, which was really a home within the castle.

Unlike the Saxony apartment, which had been left virtually untouched since the Middle Ages, Alex had modernized the rooms in his suite for day-to-day living. Still elegant enough for a king, it had all the amenities of modern-day living.

She found the spacious bathroom and showered before dressing in her blue suit. When she entered the bedroom she discovered Alex had come in. "I'm ready," she announced.

His eyes traveled over her, eventually fastening on the ring she was wearing again. "You look lovely. Where are we going?"

She blinked. "I thought you wanted me to go with you while you visited your uncle."

"You misunderstood me then. I have to be in residence at the castle in case I'm needed, but I have no intention of seeing him for quite some time.

"I asked Evelyn to keep an eye on the boys until they go to sleep so you and I could spend a little quiet time together."

His face had a gaunt look, yet for all that he was more attractive to her than ever.

"How long has it been since you had a good sleep?"

He pursed his lips. "Since the night before you came to the castle in the hope of talking to me."

She lowered her head. "I know what you mean. We're both sleep deprived."

"Phillip pointed out I have a *king*-size bed just waiting for us," he quipped. His dark mood seemed to have vanished. "If it's all right, I'd like to lie down and hold my wife for a few hours."

The blood pounded in her ears. "Aren't you hungry?"

"I had breakfast before I flew to the cabin for you. Do you want something from the kitchen?"

"No, thank you."

"Then while I change, why don't you put on something comfortable."

He disappeared into the bathroom, leaving her trembling like a leaf in the breeze.

Once she heard the door close, she was galvanized into action. By the time he emerged in a white toweling robe, she'd done his bidding and was wearing her light yellow fleece robe. One look at him left her weak.

He seemed to be waiting for something. She didn't understand when he reached for a coin. He'd left change lying next to an urn of at least three dozen red roses placed on his dresser.

"Heads or tails? It's your call."

"For what?"

"Who gets into bed first." After tossing the coin, he raised his eyes to her. "It came up tails."

"Alex—" She laughed nervously. "Don't be ridiculous."

"What did you choose?" he persisted.

"Neither one," came her meek response.

"That's what I thought."

Before she could countenance it, he picked her up in his arms and started carrying her through the suite to the outer door, not missing a breath.

"What are you doing?" Her lips accidentally brushed his hard jaw, turning her body molten. She felt the tremor that shook his powerful body before he opened the door and went out in the hall where a security guard was standing nearby.

"Alex—" She was so embarrassed she hid her face in his neck.

"I never understood the ritual of carrying the bride over the threshold, but I do now. It solves a big problem when she's terrified of her own husband."

He took her inside again and shut the door. When they reached the bed he followed her down with his body.

Darrell looked into his eyes but they were shuttered. "You know I'm not frightened of you. But I can't get my mind off your uncle. Did he have the attack before you even talked to him?"

"No. During our confrontation he ordered me to divorce you and marry Evelyn. When I refused to discuss it, he became ill."

Her eyes filled. "I'm so sorry, Alex."

"He'll be all right. In the meantime, I want to forget everything and concentrate on my wife. I need you to hold me right now. Would that be too much to ask? I'm tired of plotting and planning and trying to make everything work."

He said it with a half smile but she knew deep down he meant every word of it.

Recognizing how truly exhausted he had to be, she turned on her side and nestled in his arms with her face resting in the hollow of his shoulder.

He let out a long, drawn-out sigh, like Atlas letting go of the cares of the world. "This is heaven…." His voice trailed. He wrapped one powerful leg around both of hers, locking her in place against him. She felt him bury his face in her swath of silky gold hair.

Within a minute she could tell he was asleep.

She lay there for a good half hour while her mind tried to absorb what her body was feeling.

Every girl had times growing up when she wondered who her husband would be, how she would know he was the one.

If it hadn't been for Melissa…

With the greatest care Darrell eased away enough that she could feast her eyes on his face without him being aware of it. He had fantastic bone structure. She loved the way his hair was cut just short enough that it was still wavy.

His strong nose and chin made him aggressively male. But of all his features besides his beautiful eyes, it was his mouth she loved. Wide and sensuous, it could go fierce or tender depending on his mood.

That mouth had swept her into a vortex of desire days ago. She craved to be caught up in it again. But she would have to be patient. It was a virtue she needed to work on. For the present he required a lot of sleep without interruption.

Now that she'd been lying down for a while, she noticed the room had grown cooler because of the air-conditioning.

Inch by inch she stole out of his arms, intent on finding him another quilt. Since she didn't want to make noise opening cupboards, she went into the other bedroom and pulled one off the bed.

When she returned to their bedroom she found his long, fit body in the same position she'd left him. He was that tired.

Holding her breath, she covered him, still unable to believe she had the right to be with him and take care of him forever.

Not far from the bed there was a couch with a throw facing the fireplace. She tiptoed over to it and lay down, pulling the material up to her shoulders. There was too much temptation lying next to her husband.

Since her first flight to Switzerland, she felt as if she'd been wandering in a strange and marvelous dream. Maybe now they could both get the sleep they needed so badly. When he woke up, she wouldn't be far from him. Then maybe their marriage could really begin…

Something wasn't right. Alex had been breathing in the faint scent of Darrell's fragrance still lingering on his robe, but when he felt blindly for her, his hand didn't come in contact with warm, firm flesh covered by her modest robe.

Alarmed, his eyes opened to a room cloaked in darkness. He jackknifed into a sitting position and checked his watch. It was ten after ten. He'd slept close to ten hours!

Where had Darrell gone? Was it possible she'd acted on what she'd suggested at the cabin and had taken Phillip back to Denver?

It would be just like her to think she could fix the situation by staying out of sight.

Maybe he was getting ahead of himself and she was either in the bathroom or down in the Saxony apartment. Forcing himself not to panic he called to her.

When no answer came he was filled with dread and flung off the quilt she must have thrown over him while he slept. How long ago had that happened?

"Darrell—"

"I'm over here on the couch."

He had to stop to catch his breath. "What are you doing so far away from me?"

"I woke up a while ago and knew you needed your sleep, so I did some phoning in the other room, then came back in here to rest until you awakened."

"I was afraid you were sleeping too long and something was wrong. I—I'm so glad you're up at last."

So was he...but it was for a completely different reason.

"Are you all right, Alex? Please tell me the truth. I know you have serious issues with your uncle, but he's still family and you wouldn't be human if you weren't upset."

Alex got out of bed with the intention of joining his wife on the couch when he heard a pounding on the other side of their bedroom door.

"Dad? Mom?"

At the sound of their son's anxious voice Alex moaned, unable to believe Phillip's timing.

The need to make love to his wife was causing him physical pain. But it appeared Darrell wasn't suffering from the same problem. She switched on the light. "I'll see what he wants," she said before padding over to the door in her robe and bare feet.

Alex decided something was seriously wrong. Otherwise he knew Phillip wouldn't have disturbed them before morning. While he pulled on some boxers and retied his robe, he heard muffled voices. It sounded like Vito and Jules were out there, too.

When he opened the door to the drawing room, Jules ran over to him sobbing. "I'm so sorry, Uncle Alex. I didn't mean to drop him."

"Drop who?"

"Brutus," Vito said with tears rolling down his cheeks.

Alex's glance flew to Darrell, who was on the house phone. Phillip was standing next to her sobbing his heart out, too.

He got down on his haunches, putting his hands on Jules's shoulders. "Take a deep breath and tell me what happened."

"W-we were on the balcony and I was holding Brutus, but he kept wiggling around and all of a sudden he fell over the wall."

"Did it just happen?"

"Yes."

After another quick glance at Darrell whose pained eyes looked to him for help, he ran out of the apartment and down the stairs past his security people to the Saxony apartment. He could hear everyone running after him. The fastest way to the water was over the balcony.

Removing his robe he did a cannonball into the lake. He heard Darrell's scream just before he hit the water.

The puppy wouldn't have fallen more than a few yards from the exterior wall. Depending on its instinct to survive, it could still be paddling around, but who knew how long its strength would hold out.

It was a warm summer night. The lake was like a sheet of glass, making it easier to spot anything in the water.

"Do you see him, Dad?"

Alex kept swimming back and forth, drawing closer each time to the castle wall. Suddenly he saw something brushed up against the mossy stone.

A sleek little head and a paw trying desperately to catch hold.

With one strong lunge Alex reached the puppy whose exhausted body slumped against his shoulder. By now one of the castle patrol boats was headed toward him. Thanks to Darrell's quick thinking in calling them the puppy might have a chance to live.

They flashed a searchlight over the water. He gave a shout and waved a free hand. Quickly they came alongside and took the puppy from him before he hoisted himself into the craft.

"After you hand me a towel, call my driver to pick me up at the marina, then phone the vet and tell him I'm coming to the stable with Brutus."

Alex put the dog in the middle of the towel and began drying him as best he could. It had to survive, not so much for Phillip's sake, but for Jules's. The boy was overly sensitive like Chaz. If Brutus died, he'd never forgive himself.

If Leo were here he would say "What a hell of a night."

All Alex knew was that his heart couldn't take any more shocks.

Was it asking too much to live long enough to make love to his legally wedded bride? Only time would tell if she came to his bed willingly, but at this rate he was never going to find out!

The boat reached the marina in record time. "Here, Your Majesty." One of the men tossed him a yellow slicker to put on.

"Thank you for your help. Do me one more favor and call my wife? Tell her to meet me at the vet's office."

After that everything happened fast. Before long five people were huddled around the vet, who was examining the dog.

Alex stared at his wife who was draped in a blanket she'd

pulled from one of the beds to cover her robe. She was trying to comfort Jules, whose shoulders shook with silent tears.

"It wasn't your fault, darling. If I'd been holding him out there, the same thing could have happened. Puppies are like jelly. You can't get a good hold on them,"

Her comment made him laugh. A miracle.

The vet finally raised his head. "This little fellow has lived up to his breed's reputation. He's going to be fine by morning."

Darrell squeezed Jules. "You see? Thanks to your uncle, everything's all right." Her voice shook.

"Dad always makes *everything* all right."

When Darrell looked over at Alex, her eyes were glowing like purple fire. He couldn't get her back to the castle fast enough.

"Okay, everybody. There's been enough excitement for one night. You heard the doctor. Brutus will be back to himself after breakfast. No more holding him on the balcony. You can take him for walks, preferably on solid ground," he teased. "Let's go home and get some sleep."

"Could I stay with him tonight, Dad? I don't want him to be lonely."

The vet gave Alex a nod.

"It's up to your mother."

"Can we stay, too?" the boys asked her.

"There's no place for you to sleep."

"We don't care."

"I've got some blankets around here," the vet offered.

Alex decided it was a brilliant idea. "It's fine with me. I'll send a car for you in the morning and we'll have breakfast together."

"Hurrah!"

Darrell hurried out to the limousine ahead of Alex. When he caught up to her she said, "I think I should stay with the boys so the vet can get some sleep. As for you, a hot shower is in order." She stared at him with accusing eyes.

"That spectacular stunt you pulled off the balcony was even scarier than the one the other day. The news of this will probably make tomorrow's headlines. But please don't do it again or you'll put me in an early grave."

The fear in her voice pleased him no end. "Well, we can't have that when we haven't even gotten to the good part yet."

"There'll never be a good part if you're dead!"

On that note she clutched the blanket around her shoulders and hurried back inside the vet's office. Maybe it was a trick of light but he thought she looked paler than before. At least she still wanted him alive.

Much to the amusement of his security people, Alex returned to his apartment in the slicker and his big bare feet, hardly the attire for a king supposedly enjoying his honeymoon.

Once he'd showered and changed, he'd go back to get her, and this time there'd be nothing to stop him.

But as soon as he was ready to return to the stable, his cell phone rang. At three in the morning it could only mean trouble unless it was Darrell needing to talk.

He checked the caller ID. "Leo?"

"I heard what happened. Are you all right?"

"That depends. Darrell's not in love with me, but she married me to stay close to her son. I convinced her that Isabella deserved to find true love with someone else.

"Now I'm going to let you in on another secret no one knows about except Darrell and mother. The reason Uncle Vittorio had a heart attack was because I refused his demand that I divorce Darrell and marry Evelyn."

"Evelyn—"

"My uncle's an emotionally sick man, Leo. But I have a plan that could thwart him once and for all. It involves you."

"How?" His friend's voice sounded unsteady.

"When Uncle Vittorio comes home from the hospital in the

next eight to ten hours, he needs peace and quiet. So, I'm sending Evelyn and the boys with you to my cabin in the Upper Ungadine. It's been cleaned and stocked with provisions. Seven days ought to give you and Evelyn time to sort out your feelings, which I know have been growing over the last year. There's no man I'd rather see marry Evelyn than you."

His friend grunted. "Her parents would never approve of a nonroyal marrying their daughter."

"Times are changing. I've already set a new precedent. Uncle Vittorio will hardly be in a position to disapprove of the head of security for a new son-in-law. His silence on the subject will carry weight with her folks who want her to be happy.

"So do whatever needs doing to clear your desk, then report to the helipad by nine in the morning. I'll have Evelyn and the boys there. She'll think it's a security measure. In the meantime, no one will know where the four of you have gone."

"But, Alex—what if Evelyn doesn't want to go?"

His brows furrowed. "Then isn't it time you found out how she really feels about you, my friend?"

"Hell yes, but I have to admit I'm terrified."

"Now you have some comprehension of what I've been going through with Darrell."

"You've at least got the wedding ring on her finger."

"You mean the relic that keeps falling off? I'm afraid that's the story of our marriage so far. We haven't even had the honeymoon yet."

"Whose fault is that?"

"Like you, I'm terrified to find out."

"Give it time, Alex. It's only been a week since you met."

"I didn't need a week."

"That's what it was like for me the first time I met Evelyn. But at that point she was a happily married woman."

"That was then. You still have a whole future ahead of you. I'll be damned if I'm going to let Uncle Vittorio ruin it for either of us."

After hanging up, he summoned his driver to take him to the stable. It was past time to get his wife to himself.

Evelyn put a hand on Darrell's arm. "Could we talk for a minute before you go back to the castle?"

"Of course. It's almost morning anyway."

Darrell followed Evelyn down the stairs of the palace where they'd just put the three boys to bed. The second Evelyn had been told about the accident, she'd come to the stable insisting everyone go home to bed for what was left of the night. The puppy had gone to sleep, so there was no point staying there on the floor in the vet's office.

Evelyn ushered her in the sitting room off the foyer. The minute she closed the doors she said, "When I told you at the wedding that I was glad you'd married Alex, I really meant it. He's terribly in love with you you know."

Darrell wiped her eyes. "He couldn't be. He was just glad to have a legitimate excuse to get out of his marriage to Isabella."

"It's true he didn't love her, but he would never, ever have turned around and married you this fast if his heart weren't involved. Charles suffered over the fact that Alex would never know true happiness.

"When Alex brought you home, I saw something in his eyes that's never been there before. Trust me on this."

Darrell made a protesting sound. "It's because of Phillip. He loves him."

"That's obvious. But I'm talking about you. Even Katerina has noticed the incredible change in him. We had a talk earlier tonight. She told me my father-in-law was hoping for a marriage between me and Alex, but it would never happen under any circumstances.

"Vittorio has forgotten it takes two people in love to make a marriage work. I've met someone here I care about, too. I didn't think it was possible after Charles, but it has happened. The problem is, I'm afraid he'll never do anything about it because he's a nonroyal."

"Who is it?"

"Leo."

"He's a very attractive man," Darrell murmured. "Is there anything Alex or I could do to help things along? They're best friends."

"No. If Leo can't reach out to me the way Alex has done to you, then his love isn't strong enough. Darrell—if your feelings for Alex are as deep as I believe they are, don't hold back now. You have no idea how fearful Alex is underneath."

"What do you mean?"

"By marrying you he's done something that in ways has isolated him."

"I still don't understand."

"He's always known what he had to do to be a king in a royal marriage. But to be the husband to a woman like you is unknown territory. He and Charles used to talk about what it would be like to fall in love with a commoner.

"Even if their hearts were involved, they both agreed it could end up in disaster. No matter how strong Alex is, I know there's a part of him fearful you won't be able to handle court life and one day you'll leave him and go back to Colorado. He's very vulnerable right now."

Evelyn's observations reminded Darrell of something Alex had said last week about Phillip wanting to go home once the novelty had worn off.

But Alex was wrong then, and he was wrong now!

Excited to prove it to him, Darrell jumped up from the couch. "Thank you for the talk, Evelyn. You've helped me more than you will ever know. I need to get back to the castle. Would you do me a favor and find out where Alex is right now?"

"Of course." She picked up the phone and made an inquiry before hanging up.

"He's on his way to the vet's office."

"That's perfect. It gives me enough time for my plan to work. I need some information. Will you help me?"

Evelyn's eyes lit up. "Anything you want."

In a few minutes Evelyn's driver took her back to the castle. On the drive home Darrell's mind was bombarded with thoughts that hadn't made sense before, but suddenly everything was clear.

The Saxony apartment had been Chaz's favorite spot to get away from authority. But that little mountain cabin had been Alex's private getaway.

Their choices were very telling, especially after he'd told her he would live in a cabin in Colorado if he stepped down from the throne.

After the talk with Evelyn, Darrell was beginning to realize how much Alex had been forced to hide his real self in order to be king. Only by an accident of birth had royal duties been thrust upon him. Chaz had understood that weighty responsibility and had run from it. No doubt he'd tried to get Alex to run from it, too.

Maybe the best way to be a good wife to Alex was to find ways to make him feel like he wasn't the king when they were together. Phillip had already done that by just being himself.

Darrell was having a more difficult time of it. Twice Alex had told her his father would have approved of her. It wasn't a compliment. Not at all.

Alex could have had a princess for a wife, but in the end

he hadn't wanted one and had claimed Darrell, the farthest thing from princess material in existence.

Earlier Alex had told her he was tired of plotting and planning in order to make everything work. But *she* wasn't!

CHAPTER ELEVEN

AFTER visiting the vet's office without finding his wife, Alex had gone to the palace where Evelyn lived convinced Darrell had decided to spend the night there with the boys so she wouldn't have to face him. But she wasn't there, either.

If she wasn't ready to sleep with him, then he'd give her all the time she needed.

She'd almost married Jack so Alex had assumed she'd been to bed with him. But what if she hadn't? What if she hadn't been intimate with any man? Was it possible?

It was time to find out.

Alex returned to the castle and strode down the hall to his apartment. But he was stopped dead when he saw a note in English taped to the outer door.

Have left for the Zurich airport. In compliance with Your Majesty's wishes, I made arrangements with your pilot aboard the royal jet. Darrell.

He felt as if he'd been kicked in the gut. If she was trying to save him from himself, it was too late now.

Reaching for his cell phone, he called his pilot. "Is my wife on board yet?"

"Yes, Your Majesty. She just arrived."

"Don't you dare take off."

"She said she had your permission."

"She lied. Have you forgotten you take your orders from me?"

"No, of course not. I apologize for assuming it was all right."

"I'll be there within a half hour. Don't let her off that plane. That's a command."

"Yes, Your Majesty."

In a fury, Alex hung up and told his helicopter pilot to get ready. Five minutes later he climbed inside and gave him his instructions.

"Did you fly my wife to Zurich earlier?"

"No. You told me to wait for my orders from Leo."

That meant she'd left the palace by car and had chartered a helicopter in town, no doubt with Evelyn's help. In the process she'd sworn her bodyguard to secrecy. She could charm anyone, even his most trusted security men.

He knew she wouldn't have planned to go back to Denver if she hadn't already discussed it with Phillip. But their son was still asleep. And he didn't want to wake Evelyn again.

He gritted his teeth the whole distance to the airport. The way things were going, it was a miracle his jet was still resting there on the tarmac.

Alex jumped out of the helicopter and raced up the steps of the plane three at a time only to be stopped by another note taped to the door.

No kings allowed inside by order of the management.

What was going on in that intriguing mind of hers?

He could bang on the door, but he wasn't about to give all his security people the satisfaction of seeing him reduced to begging his wife to open up. It had been bad enough when he'd gone to her condo and she'd forced him to remain standing on her porch for what had seemed like hours.

Once again he pulled out his phone and called his pilot so he'd put Alex through to her.

She answered on the fourth ring. The wait had raised his blood pressure. At this rate *he* was due for a hospital visit.

"Alex? The captain said it was you on the line. Where are you?" She pretended to sound exhausted.

He didn't buy it for a minute, but he controlled himself enough to say, "Outside the door of the jet."

"I'm sorry to hear that. Good night."

Click.

She'd hung up on him!

Close to being in a rage he yanked on the door, expecting it to be locked. Instead it opened, causing him to almost fall from the impact of his shoulder against it.

Muttering a curse unfit for anyone's ears he headed down the passageway for his den, but she wasn't in there. The place was like a tomb.

He charged toward his mother's bedroom. It was empty.

"Darrell?"

"Do you have to make so much noise? You sound like a bull in a china shop. I'm trying to sleep."

His jaw almost cracked in response. She was in *his* bedroom. He moved to the doorway out of breath. "I want to know what you meant by your note?"

"Which one? The first note was to let you know where I went so you wouldn't worry." His eyes closed tightly. "I'm sorry if you haven't figured out the second one yet."

He folded his arms to tamp down his adrenaline rush. "I thought we had an understanding," his voice rasped.

"You mean about staying married? Of course we do, but the castle is like a hospital. You can't ever get any sleep with family, pets, staff and security men coming in and out at all hours of the night. So I thought I'd fly here and hoped the *man*, not the king, would come after me.

"As you reminded me earlier, we haven't even gotten to the good part yet. If anyone tries to find us, we'll just tell the pilot to take off."

He swallowed hard before turning on the light.

She was sitting up in the bed wearing an orange and blue pajama top that said Denver Broncos. "Good morning, my darling husband. That's what I should have said on the phone just now. It's already getting lighter in the sky so I shut the curtains."

She'd put her gleaming hair in a ponytail. There was something different when she looked at him with those violet eyes and smiled. He felt their brilliance like the blinding light after emerging from a deep black cave.

Throwing back the covers, she held out her arms. "Come here," she begged in an aching voice.

Out went the light. Like a drowning man who'd suddenly discovered sand beneath his feet and could make it to shore, he reached for her.

"Darrell—" he cried against her lips. "My love—"

"Ah, that's what I've been desperate to hear," she whispered, helping him out of his clothes. "Anything else can wait until much later."

"Did I please Your Majesty?"

After hours of lovemaking they'd both slept, but she'd awakened first and couldn't resist embracing him.

A deep groan escaped his throat, delighting her.

"Does that mean you want to be pleased again, or are you starving for food?"

"Both," he murmured against her throat, sending a thrill

through her body that set her trembling all over again. "But the food can wait. *I* can't."

"Neither can I—"

Another hour of rapture turned Darrell into a wanton. "I didn't know it could be like this—" She half lay on top of him, breathless and feverish for more.

"It isn't like this for anyone else. Thank heaven you're my wife." He kissed her with voracious hunger. "I may have to rule my kingdom from this bed."

"You won't hear any complaints from me, but everyone else who loves you might raise objections. By the way, I forgot to ask you when you first charged in here. How's Brutus?"

He chuckled into her silky hair. "Much better than I was."

"That's what I thought. You know what your problem is? You try to be too many things to too many people. You do it better than anyone I've ever known or heard of, king or no king. But now that you're my husband, I'd like you to turn all that off at the end of the day and come home to me like any other normal man."

"You can ask me that after what we've just shared?" His mouth closed over hers once more.

"You know what I mean," she said in a euphoric daze.

"Spell it out for me, darling."

"All right." She kissed his raspy jaw, loving the differences between them. "The castle is like something from a fairy tale. There aren't words to describe the fabulous world you were born into. Yet there's a part of me that also wants a home of our own."

"Done!" he cried into her hair.

"With a yard where you mow the grass and I weed the garden."

"Done!"

"And when the sink plugs up, you have to get out a wrench to fix it."

"Done!"

"Where it's not too far away so that when you leave for work every morning, you can get there in your helicopter in a big hurry."

"Done!"

"Now I know you can't really do any of that, but maybe we—"

She stopped talking. Her eyes widened as she looked at him. "What did you just say?"

"I said I love you. I said I'll grant you all those wishes. One of my homes in the next valley over would be perfect for the family we're going to raise. I knew I wanted to live there with you the moment I saw you from the doorway of the jet. I knew it when this feminine blond beauty came walking up the steps to me.

"The sun illuminated your eyes. Beyond their exquisite violet color, I saw pain, worry, sorrow, fear, incredulity—so many things that told me your true character before I even knew the exact reason for your visit to Bris. It didn't matter that you were a complete stranger to me. At that moment love hit me like a thunderclap."

"It did me, too," she confessed.

"Most people will tell you it isn't possible. They say you have to live with someone for years and years before you can call it love.

"I disagree. Love can and does happen with a mind and power all its own. By the time you left the plane to get me the ring, I'd become a different man.

"It would have been easy enough to leave things alone because I hadn't met Phillip yet. I knew he had a wonderful life with you. I could have flown away and never looked back, rationalizing that you would marry one day and supply him with a stepfather.

"But I didn't do that because I couldn't. You were there in Denver with our son. I had to see you again to find out if I'd truly lost my heart. When you gave me a hard time before letting me in your house, I determined to make you mine whether you came screaming or not."

"Oh, Alex—" She pulled his head down and began suffocating him with kisses. "While I was warming up those tacos, I had this dream that we were married and I was taking care of my wonderful husband at the end of a busy day.

"You have no idea how much I long to cook and clean for you, fold your socks in your drawers. You're everyone else's king, but you're my very heart.

"I want to have your baby. When I realized you were the man who'd made Melissa pregnant, I was horribly jealous of her, which made my guilt so much worse.

"I'm sure there'll be duties I have to perform as the king's wife, but I want to do the little personal things behind the scenes for you that no one else knows about. I also want to go to school and learn Romanche so I can be a real asset to you.

"Do you think it's possible we could combine two totally different lives and be happy?"

His sensuous smile melted her bones. "I'll let you know after we get down to the good part again."

Her heart filled her eyes. "I thought you were hungry."

"I am. For you."

"It was already better than good the first time you kissed me," she cried softly. "I was transparent that day on the mountain. I wanted you in every way a woman could ever want a man. I didn't want you to be the king. I didn't want you to belong to anyone but me."

He sobered, staring at her intently. "Chaz and I used to talk about what it would be like to find the right woman and marry her. By some miracle we both got our wish. Now I find I'm greedy and want one more miracle."

Darrell traced the line of his male mouth with her fingers. "Maybe it's already happened. I hope it has. I can't wait to feel your baby kicking inside me."

Alex drew his wife into his arms while he digested her words.

As he rocked her warm, curvaceous body against him she said, "My only concern is that your uncle will still try to turn public opinion against you for marrying me. So I think for the time being Phillip and I should go back to Colorado."

"We're married, Darrell." He crushed her against him. "Do you think I'd let you out of my sight for one second now?"

"Just until the doctor says your uncle is better. Phillip will understand. It *is* doable, darling."

He rolled her over so she was lying beneath him. "You made a vow to me before God. Did it mean nothing to you?"

Tears filled her eyes. "It meant everything. I just want to do the right thing for you. You're so wonderful, words can't express how I feel."

"Then the right thing for you to do is to go on loving me, just like this, no matter what happens."

"Is that a command?" she teased.

He struggled for breath. "No. I want you at my side, in my bed, because you want to be, and for no other reason."

"Done!"

EPILOGUE

Two months later Alex entered the conference room at the castle, nodding to Leo before looking around at his assembled cabinet. Today Alex's Uncle Vittorio had joined them.

"Gentlemen? Thank you all for coming on such short notice. I have several announcements to make.

"First of all, Uncle Vittorio has finally been given a clean bill of health, for which we're all grateful."

The room filled with applause.

"He, along with Aunt Renate, will be hosting an official engagement party for their daughter-in-law Princess Evelyn to our esteemed friend and colleague, Leo."

Thanks to Phillip who visited Jules's and Vito's grandfather on his own and had a long conversation with him, Alex's uncle had been won around by him. That had turned the tide, another miracle Alex hadn't been expecting.

"All of you will be receiving invitations. I'll leave it up to Leo to announce the date of their marriage. Needless to say, the young princes are ecstatic their stepfather-to-be was once a counter-espionage agent."

Everyone laughed, even his uncle. They all broke into enthusiastic applause, the kind that had to have lifted a weight from Leo's heart. Now for the risky part.

"Lastly, my wife and I have just learned we're expecting our second child."

The silence that followed was as palpable as the applause had been.

"Darrell would have been here with me, but she's too nauseated, so I left her at the house. You've had two months to form a consensus about me remaining king or stepping down. I'm prepared to hear what you have to say."

To his shock, his uncle Vittorio stood up. He stared at Alex for a long time. "My brother said you would make a good king." The older man who was looking trimmer because of his new diet, cleared his throat. "My brother was wrong."

Alex was waiting for the rest…

"I have it on good authority from Phillip that you are a *great* king. To quote him, 'You're the smartest man he knows. You love people, children, animals and most of all, his mom.'

"With such praise as that, may I voice my opinion first. God save the king."

While Alex stood there stunned, everyone repeated it and got to their feet clapping.

Suddenly the door opened and a wan-looking Darrell stepped inside. But her morning sickness only managed to give her an ethereal blond beauty that caused every head to turn.

How had she handled the helicopter ride? Alex's heart almost failed him. He'd wanted her here so badly. With her holding him up, he could face anything.

"May I add one more voice? God bless my beloved husband."

Silhouette

nocturne™

IT'S TIME TO DISCOVER
THE RAINTREE TRILOGY...

There have always been those among us
who are more than human...

Don't miss the dramatic first book by
New York Times bestselling author

LINDA
HOWARD

RAINTREE:
Inferno

On sale May.

Raintree: Haunted by Linda Winstead Jones
Available June.

Raintree: Sanctuary by Beverly Barton
Available July.

SNLHIBC

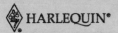

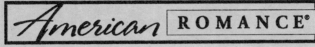

A THREE-BOOK SERIES BY BELOVED AUTHOR

Judy Christenberry

Dallas Duets
What's behind the doors of
the Yellow Rose Lane apartments?
Love, Texas-style!

THE MARRYING KIND
May 2007

Jonathan Davis was many things—a millionaire,
a player, a catch. But he'd never be a husband.
For him, "marriage" equaled "mistake." Diane Black
was a forever kind of woman, a babies-and-minivan
kind of woman. But John was confident he could
date her and still avoid that trap.
Until he kissed her…

Also watch for:
DADDY NEXT DOOR
January 2007

MOMMY FOR A MINUTE
August 2007

Available wherever Harlequin books are sold.

www.eHarlequin.com

HARM07JC

HARLEQUIN

////// NASCAR

In February…

Collect all 4 debut novels in the Harlequin NASCAR series.

SPEED DATING
by *USA TODAY* bestselling author
Nancy Warren

THUNDERSTRUCK
by Roxanne St. Claire

HEARTS UNDER CAUTION
by Gina Wilkins

DANGER ZONE
by Debra Webb

On sale
February
2007

And in May don't miss…

Gabby, a gutsy female NASCAR driver,
can't believe her mother is harping at her
again. How many times does she have
to say it? She's not going to help run the
family's corporation. She's not shopping
for a husband of the right pedigree. And
there's no way she's giving up racing!

SPEED BUMPS *is one of four
exciting Harlequin NASCAR books that
will go on sale in May.*

SEE COUPON INSIDE.

////// NASCAR

SPEED BUMPS
Ken Casper

www.GetYourHeartRacing.com   NASCARMAY

Silhouette®

Desire

They're privileged, pampered, adored…
but there's one thing they don't
yet have—his heart.

THE MISTRESSES

A sensual new miniseries by

KATHERINE GARBERA

Make-Believe Mistress

#1798 Available in May.

His millions has brought him his share of scandal.
But when Adam Bowen discovers an incendiary
document that reveals Grace Stephens's secret
desires, he'll risk everything to claim this very
proper school headmistress for his own.

And don't miss…

In June,
#1802 Six-Month Mistress

In July,
#1808 High-Society Mistress

Only from Silhouette Desire!

Visit Silhouette Books at www.eHarlequin.com   SDTM0407

REQUEST YOUR FREE BOOKS!
2 FREE NOVELS PLUS 2
FREE GIFTS!

HARLEQUIN ROMANCE®

From the Heart, For the Heart

YES! Please send me 2 FREE Harlequin Romance® novels and my 2 FREE gifts. After receiving them, if I don't wish to receive any more books, I can return the shipping statement marked "cancel." If I don't cancel, I will receive 4 brand-new novels every month and be billed just $3.57 per book in the U.S., or $4.05 per book in Canada, plus 25¢ shipping and handling per book and applicable taxes, if any*. That's a savings of over 15% off the cover price! I understand that accepting the 2 free books and gifts places me under no obligation to buy anything. I can always return a shipment and cancel at any time. Even if I never buy another book from Harlequin, the two free books and gifts are mine to keep forever.

114 HDN EEV7 314 HDN EEWK

Name _____ (PLEASE PRINT) _____

Address _____ Apt. _____

City _____ State/Prov. _____ Zip/Postal Code _____

Signature (if under 18, a parent or guardian must sign)

Mail to the **Harlequin Reader Service®:**
IN U.S.A.: P.O. Box 1867, Buffalo, NY 14240-1867
IN CANADA: P.O. Box 609, Fort Erie, Ontario L2A 5X3

Not valid to current Harlequin Romance subscribers.

Want to try two free books from another line?
Call 1-800-873-8635 or visit www.morefreebooks.com.

* Terms and prices subject to change without notice. NY residents add applicable sales tax. Canadian residents will be charged applicable provincial taxes and GST. This offer is limited to one order per household. All orders subject to approval. Credit or debit balances in a customer's account(s) may be offset by any other outstanding balance owed by or to the customer. Please allow 4 to 6 weeks for delivery.

Your Privacy: Harlequin is committed to protecting your privacy. Our Privacy Policy is available online at www.eHarlequin.com or upon request from the Reader Service. From time to time we make our lists of customers available to reputable firms who may have a product or service of interest to you. If you would prefer we not share your name and address, please check here. ☐

HR07

Coming Next Month

#3949 THE SHERIFF'S PREGNANT WIFE Patricia Thayer
Rocky Mountain Brides
Surprise is an understatement for Sheriff Reed Larkin when he finds out
his childhood sweetheart has returned home. After all these years
Paige Keenan's smile can still make his heart ache. But what's the secret
he can see in her whiskey-colored eyes?

#3950 THE PRINCE'S OUTBACK BRIDE Marion Lennox
Prince Max de Gautier travels to the Australian Outback in search of the heir
to the throne. But Max finds a feisty woman who is fiercely protective of her
adopted children. Although Pippa is wary of this dashing prince, she agrees
to spend one month in his royal kingdom.

#3951 THE SECRET LIFE OF LADY GABRIELLA Liz Fielding
Lady Gabriella March is the perfect domestic goddess—but in truth
she's simply Ellie March, who uses the beautiful mansion she is house-
sitting to inspire her writing. The owner returns, and Ellie discovers that
Dr. Benedict Faulkner is the opposite of the aging academic she'd imagined.

#3952 BACK TO MR & MRS Shirley Jump
Makeover Bride & Groom
Cade and Melanie were the high school prom king and queen. Twenty years
on, Cade realizes that he let work take over and has lost the one person
who lit up his world. Now he is determined to show Melanie he can be the
husband she needs...and win back her heart.

#3953 MEMO: MARRY ME? Jennie Adams
Since her accident, and her problems with remembering things, working in
an office can sometimes be hard for Lily Kellaway. But with the new boss,
Zach Swift, it feels different. And not just because he is seriously gorgeous!
Now he has asked her to join him on a business trip.

#3954 HIRED BY THE COWBOY Donna Alward
Western Weddings
Alexis Grayson has always looked after herself. So what if she is alone and
pregnant? Gorgeous cowboy Connor Madsen seems determined to take
care of her. And he needs something from her, too—a temporary wife! But
soon Alexis realizes she wants to be a *real* wife to Connor.

HRCNM0407